ANDY BEHRENS

DUTTON BOOKS

DUTTON BOOKS
A member of Penguin Group (USA), Inc.

Published by the Penguin Group
Penguin Group (USA) Inc., 375 Hudson Street, New York, New York 10014, U.S.A.
Penguin Group (Canada), 90 Eglinton Avenue East, Suite 700, Toronto, Ontario, Canada M4P 2Y3
(a division of Pearson Penguin Canada Inc.)
Penguin Books Ltd, 80 Strand, London WC2R 0RL, England
Penguin Ireland, 25 St Stephen's Green, Dublin 2, Ireland (a division of Penguin Books Ltd)
Penguin Group (Australia), 250 Camberwell Road, Camberwell, Victoria 3124, Australia
(a division of Pearson Australia Group Pty Ltd)
Penguin Books India Pvt Ltd, 11 Community Centre, Panchsheel Park, New Delhi - 110 017, India
Penguin Group (NZ), 67 Apollo Drive, Rosedale, North Shore 0632, New Zealand
(a division of Pearson New Zealand Ltd.)
Penguin Books (South Africa) (Pty) Ltd, 24 Sturdee Avenue, Rosebank, Johannesburg 2196, South Africa
Penguin Books Ltd, Registered Offices: 80 Strand, London WC2R 0RL, England
This book is a work of fiction. Names, characters, places, and incidents are either the product of the author's
imagination or are used fictitiously, and any resemblance to actual persons, living or dead,
business establishments, events, or locales is entirely coincidental.

The publisher does not have any control over and does not assume any responsibility for author or
third-party websites or their content.

CIP Data is available.

Published in the United States by Dutton Books,
a member of Penguin Group (USA), Inc.
345 Hudson Street, New York, New York 10014
www.penguin.com/youngreaders

Produced by Alloy Entertainment
151 West 26th Street
New York, NY 10001

Designed by Andrea C. Uva

Printed in USA
First Edition

ISBN 978-0-525-47898-0
1 3 5 7 9 10 8 6 4 2

For my dad, Leo.
Thank you.

Duncan Boone plugged his custom-airbrushed Fuego-Hammer AX50 electric guitar into an amplifier, twisted the volume knobs to their max, then flipped off the garage lights. He nodded, pleased with himself. Earlier, he had secured a dual-beam flashlight to a rafter with duct tape, angling it so it shone like a spotlight onto the garage floor. Now he stood in the light alone, listening to the amp hum. As his eyes swept over his dad's tarp-covered '65 Skylark, he imagined a rippling sea of fans in a vast arena. He triumphantly raised his arms."Thank you!" he said in an affected English accent. "Thank yooooou!"

Duncan bent a note high up the fretboard. He eased a pair of mirrored sunglasses onto his face and patted the ruffles of his oversized tuxedo shirt, letting the guitar slide low against his hip. He placed an enormous feathered hat atop his head, then tilted it forward. He cleared his throat and began to count off:

"One, two . . . a-one, two, three, four . . ."

He leapt, the plume of his hat scraping the motor of the garage door opener. Duncan began to lash at his guitar, his face contorted as though he were in unholy pain. Waves of distortion erupted from the amp. Tools rattled against the garage walls. Duncan fell to his knees. His fingers slid down the neck of the guitar, then up again. He arched backwards until the hat fell off. He jiggled the guitar lightly, as if a few notes were stuck and he needed to shake them out. More blurts of distortion. With his eyes closed tight behind the sunglasses and a haze of noise gathering around him, Duncan didn't notice the garage door beginning to rise and sunlight sweeping across the floor.

His friends Jessie Panger and Stew Varney stood in the driveway, smirking. Jessie twirled a single drumstick in her left hand. Stew bobbed his head. They watched Duncan writhe, the guitar held aloft in his outstretched arms. A small crowd of passersby began to gather, attracted (or awed, or horrified) by the crushing sounds emanating from the two-car garage on the leafy—and normally quiet—suburban Illinois street. Duncan, still using the contrived accent, began to half sing/ half scream:

> *Oh, Caa-aar-lee-eee-eey*
> *I'd eat a pound of cheese*
> *Get attacked by killer bees*
> *Hold it for an hour when I have to pee-eee*

Expose myself to hepatitis C
And pay more attention in Spanish III
If I could just get you to talk to m—

Jessie jerked the guitar cord from the amplifier.

"Sweet jam, rocker," she said flatly.

She stood above Duncan, her arms folded across a black Hüsker Dü T-shirt. Although she was a diminutive, pink-haired girl, Jessie could actually appear quite menacing. Duncan froze, lying on his back on the oil-stained garage floor with the guitar on his chest.

"Hey, Jess," he said meekly. "Just, um . . . warming up a little."

"Masterful rhymes," she said. "Really. Cheese, bees, pee . . . wow. That's powerful stuff. I think we're all smelling Grammy."

"They can't all be gems," he said. "Just freestyling a bit."

Duncan stood and removed his sunglasses. He immediately took notice of the six adults, four infants, and two Labradors gawking at him from the sidewalk.

"Hello, Mrs. Ludgin, Mrs. Marchetti. Hey there, everyone."

The kids waved frantically. The dogs wagged. The adults scarcely moved. Duncan smoothed the billowed front of his ruffly shirt and hiked up his turquoise velvet pants.

"Dude," said Stew, "you look like some sort of conquistador. But you're, like, nineteen percent more gay than other conquistadors. Not that I'm judging the lifestyles of Spanish explorers—at all. Because I'm not. That's totally not me. I mean, conquistadors can be gay, that's cool. I have total respect for gay conqui—"

"Shut up, asselope," said Jessie, smiling. "Unpack your stuff."

She placed a small box of percussion instruments—a triangle, maracas, wood blocks, a cowbell—on the garage floor, then turned toward Duncan. "Were you trying to sound British just then? And what *is* with the new look? It's kind of piratey, I think. And it's a little *Brokeback*, too. Please tell me you don't have pirate suits for the rest of the band. Peg legs and parrots, that sort of thing."

Duncan self-consciously ran his hands down the ill-fitting pants, eyed the feathered hat on the garage floor, and, without much subtlety, kicked it underneath the car.

"No parrots or wooden limbs," he said.

"Did you raid the theater-arts wardrobe closet again?" asked Jessie.

"Yeah," he said. "No way they'll miss this stuff. It's from *Twelfth Night*, freshman year. Awesome, eh?"

"Not so much, no," said Jessie. "I'm not wearing a pirate hat, Duncan."

"You think they're a little overwrought? I just thought we needed a stage presence that was more flamboyant. Nonconformist. I'd like us to stand out. I'm trying to cultivate a look that's consistent with the band's core principles."

Jessie glared. Duncan shrank slightly.

"The costumes can be optional," he said. "And I can return the hats. But they're not piratey. They're retro. Big diff—"

"Principles?" Jessie asked. "We have 'core principles'? Really? We've never even had a gig. Not one gig. We *always* stand out when we play, dude, because we're the only living things in the room." She gestured at the small dispersing group of people and pets. "*That* is officially the largest crowd that has ever seen us perform." She paused. "But please, tell me more about the Blowholes' principles."

The Blowholes were a trio of Elm Forest Township High School students—Duncan on guitar, Jessie on drums, and Stew on bass—that had formed (as a thrash-metal band called Feely Dan) in Stew's attic five months earlier. Soon after they began playing together, they moved their practices to Jessie's basement (and briefly changed their style to ska, and their name to Toby Spliff) following a series of strongly worded complaints from a nearby senior center. But weeks of basement turf battles with Jessie's eleven-year-old brother ended with a small fire and the permanent expulsion of the band (which had shifted its style to hardcore punk and its name to Velveeting Disorder) not just from Jessie's house, but—by virtue of a one-sided vote of the Glenn Oaks Estates homeowners' association—from her entire subdivision. The band next moved to the relative isolation of Duncan's garage (changing their style again to bluesy rock and their name to the Blowholes). The band, much to every member's dismay, had yet to perform in front of an audience. Getting a gig had become a critical Blowhole priority.

"Our principles," Duncan said. "Ahem. Right. Well, I've really been giving this a lot of consideration, and I'm thinking now that we're more of a concept-album band. Like Pink Floyd, maybe. But more accessible. We're like the double-album/rock opera type. We're definitely not a band that tries to churn out Top 40 singles. In fact, we *reject* the single."

"That's a new principle for the Blowholes, isn't it?" asked Jessie.

"No," Duncan said. "No, no. We just needed time to get in touch with this particular principle."

"But now you're touching it."

"Yes, I am."

"You're changing the band's name again, aren't you?" she asked flatly.

"'Fraid so," said Duncan, plugging his guitar back into the amplifier.

"But I was going to get a little spouting whale logo on the drum."

"Sorry, Jess. The Blowholes have passed into history. We are now . . ." Duncan paused for effect. "Fat Barbie."

Jessie and Stew nodded.

"It came to me during sixth period," Duncan added.

"Mandy Lubanski is in your sixth period, right?" asked Jessie.

"Uh-huh."

"She wore the unfortunate denim skirt today, yeah?"

"Uh-huh."

"Right," said Jessie. "So Fat Barbie."

"Oh, let's not attribute this to Mandy. She's a nice girl. A bit of an awkward dresser."

"Fair enough," said Stew. "So you think this name, Fat Barbie, is somehow more consistent with the—what were they again?—the 'core principles' of the band?"

"Totally," said Duncan. "It says everything we need it to. First of all, Fat Barbie is big. Obviously. Big sound, big ideas. Just big. And Fat Barbie is completely antimaterialism. Proletarian rock for the people, that's us. And Fat Barbie demands attention. We're a wake-the-neighborhood sort of band. This is our identity. These are our essential principles." He fluffed his shirt ruffles.

"The *only* principle we've ever really had," said Stew, "is your steady commitment to someday nailing Carly Garfield." Jessie snorted. Duncan grew immediately red-faced. "In fact," continued Stew, "we should just call ourselves 'Do Me, Car—'"

"Oh, shut up," snapped Duncan.

Carly Garfield had been—aside from Led Zeppelin, a short-lived flirtation with the Smashing Pumpkins, and a newfound adoration of Wolfmother—Duncan's singular obsession since the seventh grade. She was tall, smart, idealistic, unnaturally pretty, and, Duncan believed, the girl for whom he was obviously destined. He had never wavered in his devotion to her, despite the fact that she had never wavered in her apparent indifference to him.

"Don't try to cheapen what Carly and I have," he said.

"You *have* something?" asked Stew, looping the strap of his bass over his head.

"Whatever. Don't cheapen what we don't have, then. Carly

is my songwriting muse. And as such, she's as important to this band as anyone."

"I like to think the drummer is a bigger deal than the muse," said Jessie, flipping a drumstick into the musty garage air. "But whatever."

"Anyway," continued Duncan, "Carly is clearly important to me." He paused, considering the merits of having yet another Carly discussion, before reflexively saying, "And I'm not just out to *nail* her, either. What Carly and I have—or what we *will* have—is on a much higher plane than nailing. It's a kind of metapsychic connection."

Blank stares.

"She's aware of this connection, then?" Jessie asked.

"It's a little more subconscious on her end," said Duncan.

"So she's sort of invisibly, spiritually connected to you," said Jessie. "But doesn't know it yet." She sat down at the drum kit and lightly tapped a cymbal. "Well, that's clearly a problem, isn't it?"

"Not an insurmountable one," said Duncan.

"You need to take radical action," she said.

"I have a game plan."

"Really? What do you call it? The loser stalker-boy plan?" He winced. "The chick barely knows you, Duncan. Your locker is next to hers, you've weaseled your way into three of her classes—which is kinda stalky right there—and you've written, like, fifty guitar ballads about her. But she still doesn't know you exist."

"Oh, c'mon, don't be ridiculous. She knows I exist. And I've only written, like, eight ballads. That's not even a full album."

"Are you counting the Spanish songs? Like '*Mi Corazón Es Su Perro, Carly.*' Or '*Carretilla del Amor para Carly.*' Or '*Nado en Su—*'"

"Okay, no. Those were extra-credit projects. But fine. So there are fifteen songs."

"What about the Christmas carols?" asked Stew. "Like 'Heavy Metal Drummer Boy.' And 'I Saw Carly Kiss—'"

"Okay, whatever. Nineteen songs. But they aren't all ballads. Some of them kinda rock."

Jessie stared at him for an uncomfortable moment. "My point stands, Duncan. She barely knows you."

"She *so* knows me!" he protested.

"She calls you 'Dalton.'"

He winced again.

"Okay, so that's an issue to eventually address. But still, I have a game plan. It's just more of a long-term plan."

"We're juniors now, dude," Jessie said coldly. "Game's almost over."

This Duncan didn't need to be told. It was the chilling fact that kept him awake in the night. He often imagined a big digital countdown clock—the kind they use at NASA and telethons—floating above his head, noisily keeping track of days, hours, minutes, and seconds until graduation:

629:07:53:19

Tick . . . tick . . . tick. 18 . . . 17 . . . 16 . . .

When the clock finally hit zeros, as it inevitably would, Carly could go anywhere. There'd be no more sitting at lunch tables adjacent to hers, no more parking his heavily used Plymouth Reliant near her Prius in the student lot at school. If Duncan was ever going to get Carly to learn his name, which seemed like an important precursor to wooing her, he was going to have to get her to take notice of him, and soon.

"I'll admit," he said, "time does not seem to be on my side here."

Jessie shook her head. "No kidding, Duncan. That's why I'm telling you it's time for radical action. Operative word: 'action.' You need to either one, make your move, or two, forget about this chick and move on. She's just a girl, dude."

"Forget her!?" he said, incredulous. "Move on? Look, I'm willing to try almost anything, but I can't just forget Carly like she's some random crush. It's not possible. She's not just *a* girl. She's *the* girl. I mean, did John just forget about Yoko? Did Sid just forget about Nancy? Did Kurt just forget about Court-ney? No, they didn't forget."

"No, you're right," said Jessie. "Sid killed Nancy. And Kurt shot himself in the face. So I guess those could be options C and D. You want me to start writing these down?"

"That won't be necessary. But thanks. I don't think I'll be killing anyone."

"So that leaves some lesser sort of radical action. Or you could forget—"

"I am not just *forgetting* about Carly!" he snapped.

Jessie and Stew recoiled.

"Okay, so it's kind of pathetic how infatuated I am," said Duncan. "I realize that." He looked down at his feet, played a pair of random notes, then continued. "I'm way past infatuation, in fact. And I can't just turn it off. Hell, I wouldn't want to. Carly is just so . . . so . . ."

"Devastatingly hot?" asked Stew.

"Batpoop crazy?" asked Jessie.

". . . *perfect*. Carly is just definitely not the standard-issue teenage girl. She has all these amazing activist causes that she's into—"

"Creepy fringe cults," muttered Jessie.

"—she's got like a four-point-two-something GPA, so she's completely brilliant—"

"Robotic book-monkey."

"—and yeah, she's beautiful."

"Dude," said Stew. "She's like topless-Brazilian-supermodel beautiful."

"So shouldn't I follow my feelings here?" asked Duncan. "I'm only sixteen. Carly is *the* girl that I've been into for the entire into-girls portion of my life. Destiny is at work here. It's working slowly, but, you know . . . it's still at work. I *know* it." He looked at Jessie with pleading eyes. "Nineteen songs."

Jessie abruptly stood, rammed her drumsticks into a back pocket, and marched toward the open garage door with her hands upraised.

"Later, rockers. I'm not really feelin' it. The mood has gotten way too dreary in here. It's no longer a rock-conducive atmosphere." She strode off down the driveway. "For what it's worth," she called, "that little guitar solo really was all right, Duncan. The lyrics? Those need work."

Stew hurriedly packed his equipment.

"She's my ride, bro," he said. "I mean, you know I'd love to stay and jam—even if you do sound like the wussiest wuss in the Land of Wuss right now—but I've gotta catch up."

Duncan was soon alone in his garage again, pondering the only crush he'd ever really had.

2

Fat Barbie's practice was at a premature end, and Duncan felt a bit too self-aware to improvise any additional guitar theatrics. So he went inside his house, changed out of the borrowed attire, grabbed his backpack, and trudged a half mile to Watts Park, a downtown square where fashionable nannies sucked the lids of expensive mochas while crazed toddlers threw wood chips at squirrels. Watts was the social nexus of Elm Forest. Duncan's preferred location at the park was a spot near a statue of some long-dead military dude on a horse. At this approximate location, on occasional summer evenings, local bands of dubious quality would perform for large crowds of baby boomers. Duncan frequently daydreamed about rocking Watts Park with righteous and unprecedented fury, scattering the staid suburbanites and attracting a throng of thrashing punks from . . . well, he didn't know where the punks would come from, exactly—he knew only a handful personally—but the idea was still satisfying. He'd been imagining that sort of local debut since his seventh birthday, when he received his first guitar. (It was plastic, had only five strings, and was covered in Hootie & the Blowfish decals. But still, he'd loved that guitar.)

Duncan almost dragged an acoustic guitar with him to Watts that day, but decided, rightly, that on such an unseasonably warm Wednesday afternoon the park would be too packed for him to play it without attracting what was, just then, unwanted attention. So he merely sat by his grim soldier-with-horse statue, zipped open his backpack, and withdrew a collection of textbooks and spiral binders. He fanned them out on the grass, then reached for a binder on which he'd re-created the cover of Zeppelin's *Physical Graffiti* in Sharpie and crayon. But in place of the album title, he'd written "AP English Journal." His honors English teacher, Mrs. Kindler—a slight woman who seemed to be addicted to turtlenecks, wool pants, and glass animal figurines—required a certain amount of monthly journaling on ostensibly any subject, but preferably on the course's assigned reading. Duncan generally found this to be painless homework, the sort of thing he could still manage to slog through when he felt incapable of functioning academically. In fact, he'd begun to like it. He'd never maintained a journal or a diary before, and his MySpace page was moribund and less than revelatory. But there were things he couldn't adequately work through in song lyrics, so he appreciated having the journal as an outlet. This wasn't something he cared to reveal to Mrs. Kindler, though.

He idly skimmed earlier journal entries, then arrived at a blank page. He doodled a few ideas for the band's logo, fretted briefly about Barbie trademark infringement issues, and then began to write.

I'd just like to say—and not for the first time in these pages—that forcing your students to maintain a journal of their private thoughts, and then to actually GRADE them on those private thoughts is, in a word, fascist. Deeply fascist, Mrs. Kindler. I should write only lies. You're lucky I need the grade. And worse than the fascism is the fact that we're actually KEEPING A HANDWRITTEN JOURNAL at all! What am I, Percy Shelley? I mean really. Three-fourths of us have blogs, Mrs. Kindler. The 21st century says hello. Anyhoo . . .

Costumes for the band = epic disaster. I suppose it could've gone worse, but I'm not sure how. Stew thought I looked like a Spanish explorer. Maybe I did. If we were a flamenco ensemble, this would be great. For the purposes of Fat Barbie it was not. So I'm back to redesigning the band's onstage aesthetic. If we ever get ourselves onstage, the proper aesthetic is important. Clearly. In non-wardrobe band news, I've worked out a nifty chord structure for "Rabid Gibbons at the Country Club." Like you care. But it rocks. Again: like you care.

Here, just to satisfy a pseudo-requirement of this fascist project (JK! with the fascist-stuff. Sort of): the sheer amount of deceit taking place in *Gatsby* is impressive in one way, insane in another. This is the most wholly unlikable cast of characters in anything I've ever read, I think (with the possible exception of *The Scarlet Letter,* 'cuz Puritans suck, and the sooner English teachers figure it out the better). The dishonesty, the manipulation, the crazy-rich people . . . there's a little West Egg/East Egg thing in Elm Forest, I guess. But God. It's all so bleak and horrible. Should you be letting us read this sort of thing, Mrs. K? Isn't the average American high school student already overexposed to the hollow lives of the obscenely rich? *Cribs, My Super Sweet 16,* et cetera? I'm pretty sure I'm overexposed, at any rate. We're supposed to identify with the narrator, Nick, right? I kind of do, I guess. But wish I didn't.

Duncan briefly lifted his head from the page. He rubbed his eyes. He watched a pair of skateboarders repeatedly fail to land every trick they attempted. He saw a wrinkly man coax a pigeon onto his arm with bread crust. He watched a fleshy woman shuffle toward a water fountain, a giant leather purse swinging at her side, and wondered briefly if Mandy Lubanski would be willing to dance around onstage for Fat Barbie. Then, across the sloping field of Watts Park—by the Himalayan-themed play structure made from recycled plastic— he saw her: Carly Garfield.

Perfect, he thought.

She was luminous. She was angelic—like with harps play- ing and cherubs flitting around. Her perfect brown hair was pulled up in a neat bun. Her perfect white teeth gleamed as she joked with a gaggle of friends. She wore a perfectly snug- fitting yellow T-shirt and perfectly cut-off jeans that suggested, Duncan imagined, other perfect stuff. This didn't happen often, a random Carly encounter outside school. It was to be appreciated. She seemed to move in a kind of slow motion, out of step with the imperfect world around her. Duncan was paralyzed by the sight of her. Somewhere in the far-off rational wing of his mostly Carly-focused brain, a voice echoed.

"You need to take radical action," it said.

Instead, he stared. His pulse accelerated. The journal slipped from his lap and onto the grass. He didn't reach for it. Carly stood among her friends—all of them subordinate crea- tures, like handmaids—and seemed to be explaining something to them while gesturing at various objects in the park. They were maybe half a football field away, Duncan thought, based on his limited knowledge of football fields. He couldn't quite hear what Carly was saying amid the playground sounds, but he definitely enjoyed watching her say it. The handmaids listened intently. They each seemed to be carrying a pile of pink flyers. Carly extended her long, perfect arm, then let it sweep across the park in a semicircle, stopping to point at . . .

Duncan emitted an audible gasp, startling a group of nearby pigeons into flight.

Carly seemed to be pointing *directly* at him. He nearly convulsed. An agitated pigeon pooped on Duncan's journal. He failed to notice. He was completely transfixed. It was possible, he thought, that Carly was merely pointing at the statue. Or at the clearing where the lousy bands played. Or maybe beyond the park entirely. But it also seemed possible, just at that instant, that she was pointing specifically at Duncan.

His breathing became quick. He couldn't move. Carly appeared to wave her hand just slightly. Duncan involuntarily waved back—an exaggerated dork-spasm of a wave that elicited a snicker from at least one of the handmaids.

Duncan gasped again, sensing that he'd made a tactical error.

"Oh, crap," he said. "Crap, crap, crippity-crap. Crap." You don't gesture back unless you know—unless you stone-cold *know*—that you were the target of the original salutation. "Ack," said Duncan. "Stupid, stupid, stupid . . ."

Carly leaned her head to the side, evidently taking notice of the jittery boy near the statue for the first time, and not quite knowing who he might be. Duncan bent low, hiding his face, suddenly hoping—desperately—to go unrecognized. "It's never been a problem for her before," he mumbled. He began to sweat. A lot. He fumbled with the pen in his hand, drumming it nervously on his leg. Then he decided to flee.

Duncan hastily gathered his things and stuffed them into the backpack, again not noticing the pigeon excrement. He didn't dare look up. He needed simply to escape this moment, he'd decided. Flustered, he flung the unzipped backpack over his shoulder. *The Great Gatsby* and two pens flew out, landing in a four-spouted drinking fountain. Duncan retrieved the book and left the pens. He quickly took a drink, hoping to convey just the sort of casualness that he didn't possess.

"You need to take radical action," repeated the voice in his head. This time, it cruelly ridiculed him.

"I need to leave in a big-ass hurry is what I need," he answered, still mumbling. "Leave, leave, leave . . ." He was in a full panicked retreat. He thought he heard laughing at the opposite end of Watts Park as he strode away.

"Dammit, dammit, dammit . . ."

He left the park heading entirely the wrong direction. Part of him wished he could just keep moving along that vector, traveling the entire 24,900-mile circumference of the Earth (give or take, as he'd learned in sophomore geography) if necessary in order to ensure that he would absolutely, positively *not* be identified by Carly and her herd. But instead, he merely traveled a block past the park and then reversed course, remaining on the perimeter of Watts at a reasonably safe distance. He looked back periodically to watch Carly, who had moved closer to the statue, continue to describe God-knew-what to the handmaids. She stood in the grass near the apex of the Watts slope, gesticulating with great enthusiasm. Duncan, disgusted at his own pathological ineptitude, ducked his head and walked home.

Thwung. Thwung. Thwung...

Duncan pounded his head lightly against his metal locker. Number 535, near the computer lab. His eyes were shut. He made no effort to open the locker. He knew everything that was in there, where it sat, and how it got there.

Thwung. Thwung. Thwung...

Kinda like a kick drum, he thought.

It was 6:37 a.m. on Thursday, more than an hour before first period. Duncan had arrived at school uncharacteristically early in order to achieve something that was, at least for him, entirely new: he wanted to avoid Carly. He was not quite over the park episode. Carly's locker was directly next to his. Number 533. It smelled vaguely like oranges.

Thwung. Thwung. Thwung...

Back in early September, Duncan—acting through intermediaries—had negotiated a series of locker trades in order to situate himself near Carly. At the time he considered this an astonishing coup. In exchange for something like two hundred prestamped hall passes (his mom was a guidance counselor) and copies of Jessie's sophomore year geometry quizzes (she was a math freak), Duncan managed to orchestrate a six-person locker swap, making it appear as if the entire thing had been a plot by several wrestling cheerleaders to move near Albert Trejo, state finalist in the 112-pound weight class. And who suffered because of the locker rearrangement? No one. Certainly not Albert. Not Carly, either. Duncan had hardly spoken to her.

Thwung. Thwung. Thwung . . .

Yup, the park incident was deeply troubling, he thought. A serious setback. Even though it was entirely possible that neither Carly nor her flock identified him as the waver, he decided he was going to lie very low for a while. He'd collect everything he needed for his prelunch classes, then spend the rest of his morning in the resource center. Or in the cafeteria. Or in his car. Or in the woodshop breaking his toes in a vise. Basically, he didn't care where he was, as long as he risked no further embarrassment in front of Carly.

But first, just a bit more ritualized punishment.

Thwung. Thwung. Thwu—

"You know, repetitive head trauma is really bad for you. I read an article." Duncan's eyes flashed open. He turned and saw Jessie skipping down the second-floor hallway. "That's why soccer players are such goofs. All those balls bouncing off their heads. It's just not good for people. Blunts their young minds. Basically you don't want to hit stuff with your head unless it's absolutely necessary." She hopped to a stop beside him. "And c'mon, when is it ever really necessary to hit stuff with your head, Duncan? Never."

He smiled.

"Good morning, sunshine. You're here early."

"Yup, sure am. I'm beginning my school day just like I'll end it: sitting in detention, carving things on a desk."

"Detention? Still? Because of the Tater Tot assault on that yearbook chick?"

"No, no. The erotic noises at the volleyball assembly."

"Oh, right. That was nice. I thought it was pretty hot, actually."

"Just trying to inspire the team. Go Owls. Hoot." She shrugged. "Hey, sorry to bail on practice yesterday. I'm kind of a hothead, I guess. And you were kind of . . ."

". . . pathetic. Totally, unforgivably, girl-obsessed, flagrantly pathetic."

"Right. That."

"Yeah, it got worse after you left."

"It got *worse*? What could you do that was more pathetic? Sing Michael Bolton songs? Make out with a secret inflatable Carly doll? Put on some Mariah Carey and sob deep, womanly sobs?" She pouted, then mockingly stroked his arm. "Poor widdle Dunky-poo."

"*No*," he said emphatically. "And there is no secret doll. But don't give me any ideas." He banged his head against the locker again and said, "I went to Watts. Did a little homework. Carly was there. I waved at her—a total geek wave. You should've seen this wave. Unbelievable. God, I'm an idiot."

"You waved at her." Jess drummed her fingers against a locker.

"Yeah. Stupid, I know."

"Um . . . huh? Why was it stupid to wave at her?"

"Dude, this was such a spazzy-ass wave. It's almost indescribable. Totally stupid."

"I fail to see how any wave, no matter how spazzy, is worse than my hypothetical scenario where you make out with an inflatable doll. Are you really so screwed up over this flakeball that you can't even deal with *not giving her your best wave?*" She stared for a moment. "Look, you know those creepy loner kids who no one ever notices until they stash a bomb under their coat and blow up a lunchroom? Well, to Carly, you're like one of those guys. Before the atrocity." Duncan gave her a puzzled stare. "Dude, what I'm saying is this: you would literally have to *blow crap up* around here in order to get her to notice you. So don't sweat the park." She slugged his arm, and not softly. "Later. I've gotta go serve my time."

Jessie whistled and air-drummed as she bounded off toward wherever it was detentions were served—Duncan, when he broke rules, tended to break them in a more subtle manner than her. His behavioral record was thus far unblemished.

He stood in the silent white-tiled hallway and considered the possibility that—even if Carly and her friends had noticed him at the park—they were over it yesterday. Whatever snickering they did at his expense probably didn't last very long. After all, the significance of Duncan (or Dalton) Boone in the life of Carly Garfield was not quite the same as the significance of Carly Garfield in the life of Duncan Boone. He sighed, leaned against the locker, and allowed himself a small laugh.

Then he heard Carly's unmistakable voice from the stairwell, and the clap of her sandals against the floor. These were unexpected sounds—they were difficult to process. Duncan watched Carly turn down the hallway toward her locker. He admired the swish of her patchwork hippie skirt. He stared for several seconds before a small voice from within stammered, "Oh, crudballs."

Then the voice demanded to know what the effing F she was doing at school.

Normally, prior to six forty-five, the halls offered nothing but a few strays: school-district maintenance employees, chronic detention-servers like Jess, and tired jocks getting ready to practice God-knew-what. Carly Garfield arrived at seven twenty-five like clockwork—no, like cesium atomic clockwork. She did *not* arrive at . . .

"Oh, *crudballs!*" repeated the voice, this time in desperation.

Carly was no more than sixty feet away and closing fast. She was sipping an organic cola and chattering with what appeared to be the same handmaids from the park. Duncan spun around to face his locker, then began to twist its dial with unnecessary haste. He tried to focus on the details of the Carly/handmaid dialogue.

Carly: ". . . and that's a big if, but *if* we get that kind of support from the national organization—which is completely loaded right now because Bill Gates or Oprah or Bono or some bazillionaire just gave them a bazillion dollars—then this could be completely . . ."

Handmaid Number 1: "So, like, *Bono* might be there? In Elm Forest? That'd be sooo cool."

Carly: "No, Marissa, I'm not saying he'll *be* there. I'm saying that's how rich these guys are. They're Bono-rich. Oprah-rich."

Handmaid Number 2: "Ohmygod, if Oprah's there, my mom will wet herself. She's a total Oprah junkie. An Oprahzoid. An Oprahphile. An O—"

Carly: "No, Oprah is *not* going to . . ."

Duncan tugged at his lock, which didn't open. He'd been too frantic and too zeroed-in on Carly's conversation to precisely turn the dial. Again, almost involuntarily, he banged his head. Hard.

Thwung!

At this, the girls stopped talking.

A deeply uncomfortable quiet replaced their discussion. Seconds passed. The idea had been *not* to attract attention, and *not* to be noticed by Carly and her entourage. Duncan couldn't look anywhere but at his lock. He felt sweat begin to bead across his forehead. He tapped his foot nervously. Gaining access to his locker seemed—ludicrously and incorrectly—like the singular way to escape the tension of moment. He jerked open the lock.

But the awful silence persisted.

Duncan hurriedly removed the books and notes required for his morning classes, placed them on the floor, and, using both hands, crammed his overstuffed backpack into the narrow locker. He was certain that Carly and her coterie of underlings were watching, giggling quietly. He bent down to collect his books. A drip of sweat splatted on the floor. He stood up, shut the locker with a nudge, then turned to escape down the hallway. But Carly stood in his path with a half-perplexed look on her face.

"Oh, hey," said Duncan, flustered yet unable to endure any more unnerving quiet.

She nodded in an almost undetectable way.

"How's, um . . . yeah . . . how're you?" Duncan stammered.

"Great," she said softly, tilting her head and smiling.

The handmaids looked at Duncan with blank eyes. Carly simply stood there, a polite grin on her face. Duncan continued sweating.

"So, um . . . ready for that exam in Mr. Arnold's class?" he asked. "I don't know if I ca—"

"Oh, I'm ready," she said, still smiling.

"Right. Of course." He returned the smile. "I mean, you're usually ready for tests and whatnot."

Duncan stared at Carly's T-shirt. It featured a cartoon of a terrified gerbil-like creature strapped to a lab table, getting jolted by fat bolts of electricity. The shirt read T.A.R.T.S. across the top and, below the image, "SHOCKED?"

Upon realizing that he'd been eyeing Carly's chest for several seconds, Duncan enthusiastically and awkwardly proclaimed, "Cool shirt! The Tarts. Very cool. Is that a band?"

"No," Carly said. "It's an acronym."

"Cool," said Duncan. "I love acronyms."

"It stands for 'Teens Against Rodent Test Studies,'" she continued. "We're not a band, we're a cause. You don't think torturing animals is cool, do you?"

"Um . . . no. Gosh. No, no. Emphatically this time: *No*. Certainly not." He shook his head. "I mean, I lost total respect for Ozzy when I heard about all the bat-eating. That's so gross." Carly gave him a puzzled look. He continued. "But of course bats aren't technically rodents, are they? No. They're, um . . . well, I really don't know what they are. Fuzzy brown cave dwellers." More sweating. "They're kind of icky, really. Not that rodents are such hotties, either. Heh." Carly didn't quite laugh. Duncan kept prattling. "Of course that doesn't mean they should be tortured. Ever. Personally, I have never tortured a rodent. That's one thing about me that you can pretty much take to the bank. Duncan Boone: friend to the rodent community. That's me in a nutshell."

Carly smiled again, then glanced at the books in Duncan's arms.

"Looks like you've got a little bird dooky on your journal there," she said.

He peered down at the white splotch of encrusted bird poop that covered the upper-right corner of the journal.

"Hmm," he said. "So I do."

Duncan felt a surge of anxiety. His hands grew suddenly chilly. He tried to appear calm while examining the splotch.

"It looks kinda like Wisconsin, don't you think?" he said. "See, there's Door County. And there's Madison. That'd put Sheboygan right abou—"

"Looks pretty much like a bird dooky to me," Carly said.

A handmaid twittered.

"Yup," said Duncan. "No denying it." He paused. Duncan was flushed and nearly breathless. "Well," he managed, "I suppose I'd better clean it up a little before I hand it in to Kindler, eh?" He laughed a defeated laugh.

"Yup, guess so," Carly answered.

Duncan bowed his head and walked toward the stairs.

"'Bye, Dalton."

4

Duncan spent the remainder of his school day in a fog of disgust and disbelief. During gym he took a soccer ball to the face and another off his ass. He forgot to change out of his rancid, too-tight EFTHS OWLS PHYS. ED. shirt after class. He answered every question in Spanish with either *"No sé"* or *"No entiendo,"* then did the same in Physics to the amusement of his class and the befuddlement of his teacher, Dr. Wiggins. At lunch he merely poked at his taco casserole with a cafeteria spoon, and shrugged or grunted in response to Jess and Stew. They attempted to cheer him up by softening their position on pirate hats specifically, and lavish costumes in general. But it was useless. Duncan arrived minutes late to all his afternoon classes, as there was absolutely no way that he was going to endure a between-class encounter with Carly. Not that day. Nuh-uh.

All in all, it was a lost Thursday spent in contemplative self-loathing.

When the PA chime that signaled the end of eighth period went off, Duncan—having already collected his backpack—trudged toward the nearest exit, not passing by his mom's office in the guidance counselor's lair, not connecting with Jess before her second detention of the day, and *definitely* not going within five hundred feet of his own locker.

He ambled down the long, unnecessarily curving pathway that led to student parking lot A, then sighed as he saw his battered blue Reliant parked only two spots away from Carly's pristine new yellow Prius. A small plastic dolphin hung from her rearview mirror. Duncan passed behind the cars and glanced at Carly's array of bumper stickers:

BUY ORGANIC

NO NUKES FOR YOU

MURDER, IT'S WHAT'S FOR DINNER (This had a picture of a frightened cow.)

NO FRANKENFOOD

TARTS: PETS, NOT TESTS (This featured the gerbil-like thing from Carly's shirt being chased by a syringe.)

END INTERNAL COMBUSTION

OWLS GIRLS' BASKETBALL PRIDE: PASS, SHOOT, SCORE (This had a picture of an owl in a headband, shorts, and high-tops. Which seemed cruel.)

There a was also a stack of STEAL THIS SUV stickers visible in the rear window. For a brief moment Duncan allowed himself to imagine Carly in camouflage gear and face paint, surreptitiously placing these on Cherokees, Hummers, and Expeditions in some mall parking lot. He smiled at the thought. Then he remembered the fact that she must think he was a soulless, insensitive imbecile, and the smile faded. He sank into the once-plush seat of the aged Reliant coupe and drove out of the lot, winding aimlessly through the streets of moderately affluent Elm Forest, Illinois—which hadn't had elms in decades, or a forest—and into neighboring Maple Grove—sparse maples, no groves—where he stopped at Guitar Vault to price pedal tuners. He bought only replacement strings and picks, then drove home along an indirect route.

When he arrived at his family's two-story house, he saw his eleven-year-old sister, Talia, in the front yard with her obnoxious, hog-snouted neighbor friend Emily. Duncan slid out of the car with great effort, heaving his backpack over his shoulder.

"Hey, Dunk!" chirped Talia.

"Hello, T," he said, tapping her head and attempting—but failing—to smile.

"Hey, dork!" said Emily, chortling.

"Hello, creature from sub-Hell. Troll. Cretin. Slug-eater. Witch baby. Always nice to see you around the yard corrupting my sister."

"*Duncan!*" said Talia, appalled. "I'm so sorry about him, Emily."

"You're weird, dork," said Emily. She crunched a mouthful of Nerds. "Gonna practice sucking at guitar tonight? 'Cuz you don't quite suck enough. What's the name of your band anyway, dork? The Rolling Sucks? Suck Daddy? Death Cab for Sucky?"

He walked slowly up the front walk.

"Hmm. Those aren't bad, nose-picker. Not bad at all."

He slammed the door shut. His mom's keys and purse were on the table in the foyer. He heard distant kitchen sounds. Although he had hoped to escape any idle post-school-day conversation with his parents, his mother beckoned.

"Duncan Michael Boone!"

He heard the grinding of the electric can opener, then the pop of a jar lid, then the chopping of something. Meat-loaf-and-asparagus night was under way. He loped toward the kitchen.

"Yes, Katherine Hildegard Boone." He sighed plaintively. "How can I assist you?"

"My middle name is not Hildegard, Duncan."

"Whatever. I'm here to serve." Sunlight through the window reflected off sudsy water of the sink, sending waves of light and shadow over the walls.

"Isn't it an amazing day? Cripes' sake, it's almost October. Can you believe this weather? It hit eighty-five today."

"Low sixties by the weekend, they say. Maybe rain. Pretty soon it's freezing rain. Ice on the roads. Pileups on the express-way. Angry shoveling at dawn. Chicago weather, Mom." He fell onto the yellow vinyl seat of a tall metal chair.

"What compels a sixteen-year-old boy to pay attention to the weather, anyway? Really, Duncan. You're too serious."

"I'm a brooding musician, Mom."

"Right. There's big money in that, honey. Companies are always looking for good brooders. A critical corporate skill." She furiously hacked at stalks of asparagus, sending green shrapnel to the floor.

"Why am I here, Mom?" He folded his arms on the circular glass kitchen table, then rested his head.

"That's a profound existential question, sweetie pie. Why *are* you here? Why are any of us here? Are we merely the by-product of thirteen billion years of accidental subatomic cohesion, or is there a greater purpose to things, some guiding han—"

"The *kitchen*, Mom. The kitchen is what I meant. Why am I in the kitchen? You called me in here. Why am I here watching you chop asparagus? I'm a high school student. I have tests, quizzes, homework, attention deficit problems, video games that make me violent—I have things to do, Mom."

"Oh, right. I just haven't gotten to see you today, sweetheart." She looked up from her cutting board and smiled. "You left so early this morning. And you didn't stop by my office after school. I was worried. Thought you might have joined a gang."

"I think we both know that I would not be an asset to a gang."

"You're a well-liked young man, Duncan. And an excellent student when you apply yourself."

"Yeah, um . . . I'd guess those are not the traits that gangs actively seek, Mom. I'm not really much help in a fight. Anyway, I don't know of many Elm Forest gangs, so it's not an issue right now."

"I spoke with Dr. Wiggins in the faculty lounge today."

"Boundaries, Mom. It's important that we establish boundaries at school—and maintain them. I don't need you hitting up my teachers for unscheduled updates."

"Oh, relax. He just mentioned to me—without my soliciting any update on your progress, or lack thereof—that you were responding to him in Spanish today." She rested the knife on the countertop and plopped the asparagus spears into a pot of water. "I thought that was sort of interesting. And horrifying. And embarrassing to me at every possible level, both personally and professionally." She hummed softly.

"Yeah, well." His head sank deeper into his crossed arms. "I'm supposed to be practicing my conversational Spanish."

"Just maybe not in Physics class. There you should be learning about falling objects, kinetic energy, protons or photons—that kind of thing." She placed the pot on the stove, then walked over the kitchen table and stroked Duncan's hair. "Are things okay at school, honey? Is something bothering you? Are you being pestered? Is it girl trouble?"

"Yes, Mom. That's it. Girl trouble. And pestering. Girls are pestering me, in fact. I can't shake 'em. They follow me everywhere. They cry out my name. 'Duncan!' they say. 'We love you!' It's horrible, Mom. The pom girls are the worst. Oh, the poms, Mom."

"We don't have to discuss what's bothering you, Duncan. But you don't have to make a joke of everything, either."

"Boundaries, Mom."

"Right."

They sat in silence for a while. Duncan remained slumped over the table. Eventually, he spoke in a low mumble.

"That Emily Axelrod girl—the little imp with the French braids and the shrill voice and the potty mouth—is playing out front with Talia. You've got to break that up, Mom. She's trouble. Take an interest in your daughter's life." Another sigh. "Mine is beyond repair."

Bubbling sounds began to emerge from the pot.

"Ah, yes. The grim self-obsession of youth. You certainly are a brooder, dear."

She went to the stove to stir the asparagus.

"Thanks for the talk, Mom." He stood slowly. "I can see why you went into the guidance arts."

"Treat your mother nicely." She stirred.

"Sorry." He sighed again. "I'm going out to the garage."

"Of course you are. Did Jimmy Page have to practice this much?"

"Actually, he dropped out of school when he was sixteen. And now he's worth like a quarter of a billion dollars or something." He grinned broadly at his mom. "Whadya make of that?"

"Oh, I'm sure that's pretty much how it goes for every boy who drops out of high school to play the guitar. A few years go by and—poof!—suddenly they're millionaire rock superstars with planes, limos, country estates. I'm sure they almost never end up addicts or convicts or poverty-wage retail employees." She smiled back. "Velma Ludgin says you were quite the little virtuoso yesterday, rolling around on the floor, guitar blaring."

"Good *Gawd*. Mrs. Ludgin saw only the smallest snippet of a work in progress. It's not fair for her to evaluate me." He approached the screen doors that led to the backyard. "Plus the Ludgins are all churchy. Velma doesn't approve of my band. Thinks we're devil worshippers."

Duncan slid the door open wide, then stepped out onto the sunny patio.

"Your father will be home around six thirty," called his mom.

"If he weren't, I'd suspect foul play."

Duncan pulled a small silver phone from his pocket and speed-dialed Jessie.

"Hey, it's J. Leave me a message. Or don't. I'll still know that you called. And it's rude not to leave a message when I know you called, so just do it, loser."

This was followed by an androidal voice that also asked him to record a message, then by a lengthy beep.

"Hi, Jess. Duncan. It's, like, five something-ish. Just calling to see . . . I dunno . . . if you've been rehabilitated by detention. Or maybe it's made you more violent and lawless. We just read about that in my Psych class. Call me back. I'm gonna mess around with the practice setup, then have meat loaf with the family." He paused. "I bet Carly wouldn't approve of meat being mashed up into loaves, would she? No, she proba—"

Another beep and the recording cut off. He snapped the phone shut and returned it to his pocket, took four steps down the flagstone walk that led to the garage, then heard Jessie's ringtone—Zeppelin's "No Quarter"—begin to play.

"Hey, Jess."

She said nothing.

"Hello? Jess?"

She cleared her throat.

"Do you know why I didn't answer your call just then?"

"Um, because you were passionately entangled with your detention monitor, Mr. Moiaki? Or maybe you were. . ."

"Wrong, flunky. I was *ignoring* you. That's right: ignoring you. And do you know why?"

"Um, because you think that by playing hard to get I'll finally ask you to be my best gal? Or may—"

"Wrong again, chucklehead. I was ignoring you because you couldn't manage three words to me and Stew at lunch today, dude. Not three words. What was *with* you? You were, like, the undead. A zombie. A friggin' vegetable. What kind of band do we have if we can't communicate, Duncan?"

"Sorry. I know. Very sorry. I had, um . . . well, you know how you said that my punk-ass wave at the park was really no big deal, that it wouldn't really register with Carly the way it did with me?"

"Yeah, I do." She sounded exasperated.

"Well, she showed up at her locker right after you left for detention. I'm pretty sure I successfully made a lousy-yet-memorable impression this time. I kinda made fun of her do-gooder club. Then I had poop on my notebook."

"Poop?"

"Not mine. A bird's. But it was definitely poop. She pointed it out."

"So she talked to you?"

"Yeah, about the poop on my English journal. Not one of my better moments. I fell into a funk. A malaise. Torpor. A lang—"

"Okay, thesaurus-pants. I get it. You stink at girls."

"Something like that."

"I'm coming over."

Click.

Duncan fussed in his garage for a while, attaching multi-colored lights to overhead beams, adjusting and positioning amplifiers, writing out set lists of the band's half-finished songs for gigs that didn't exist. After fifteen minutes or so, Jessie arrived. She shot into the garage through a side door, drummed a bit on a case of motor oil, then sat atop a work-bench.

"So you're ready to play, yeah? No more enviro-girl dis-cussion, right? In this garage, the band's the thing. In this garage, we rock."

And, for about ninety seconds, they did, blitzing through a Strokes medley. Jessie punctuated the warm-up with an almost hostile drum flourish. Duncan smiled.

"Have you ever considered lining your drums with

tinfoil?" he asked while fiddling with an amp. "It sounds crazy, I know. But I read John Bonham used to do it."

"Interesting. And that would make me louder?"

"It might. He was loud."

"Sweet—maybe I will. I heart loud." She tapped her right foot. "C'mon, let's play s'more. I've been a prisoner all day. How 'bout 'Chain-Smoking Floozy' on my count, okay? One, two, a-one, two, thr—"

"Oh, wait. I've gotta finish telling you about the incident this morning with Carly. First of all, can you friggin' believe she got to school before seven? Blew my mind. And then she jus—"

Jessie whipped a drumstick into Duncan's ribs like she was Link with a boomerang.

"Hey!" He grabbed his side, wincing. "What was *that* for?"

"We are *not* discussing that flakeball!" She hurled a cowbell at his head, narrowly missing. "I've got a boxful of small instruments over here that can be thrown at high velocity, dude, and I'm unloading 'em on your sorry punk ass until you swear—until you take an *oath*—that you will not discuss that chick anymore today."

"Fine, but I . . ."

She flung a maraca at his midsection. He deflected it with his guitar. It landed rattling on the Skylark's tarp.

"Dude! Chill!"

"I'm serious, Duncan! No more crap about Carly! I am *not* the sit-and-listen, tell-you-that-you're-special sort of girl!"

Her pink hair flew as she scolded him. "That's not my thing. Don't whine to me about this chick, okay?"

"It's just that I . . ."

She sidearmed a steel triangle, catching him in the right shoulder.

"Owww!"

"Take the oath!" She lowered her voice to sound slightly more Duncan-y. "'I, Duncan Boone, will not discuss Carly Garfield in the presence of Jess Panger, rock goddess, until she gives me permission to do so.'"

"All I was gonna say . . ."

She fired another maraca, this time nailing him square in the forehead.

"Boom, suckah!" shouted Jessie, grinning.

Duncan stepped forward, his eyes closed and his right hand rubbing his head.

"Okay, I give! This is me, taking the oath. I, Duncan Boo—"

It happened in mere seconds, but to Duncan it felt like a stop-action sequence that lasted minutes: first, his foot landed on one of the roller-things his dad used to wheel himself under cars; then the roller-thing spun away, flipping Duncan backward like a diver off a platform; next he crashed into an unstable shelving unit and landed, butt-first, on the concrete floor.

An old stereo speaker was the first thing to hit him in the head. The shelving unit and all its contents teetered for a moment, then fell directly onto a sprawled-out Duncan. Glass shattered; wood splintered. Somewhere at the bottom of the heap of garage detritus, Duncan moaned.

Jessie sprang up from the drum kit and quickly began to dig him out, alternately apologizing and cursing. "Totally sorry, dude . . . so sorry . . . but damn, it was just a *maraca*. Who can't take a maraca to the head? I mean, seriou—"

She stopped midword when she lifted the speaker up and saw his face.

"Ho. Lee. *Crap*." Her mouth was agape as she looked at Duncan. His lip was bloodied, his left eye had already begun to swell, and a gash had been opened across the bridge of his nose. "Dude," managed Jessie. "It was a *maraca*."

He moaned again.

"Speaker got me," he said groggily. "Then the hundred-twenty-five-watt amp. Then a die-cast Starship *Enterprise*, then the clay Hillary Clinton I made for my dad in fifth grade." Another moan. "Can't believe he keeps that in the garage . . . thought he loved it." Duncan rubbed his head.

"We've gotta get you inside, dude," said Jessie. "You'll probably have a pretty sweet shiner. And you're bleeding like Rocky in . . . well, like Rocky in every Rocky movie."

"Perfect end to a perfect day," he groaned.

5

"Dude, your mom was *pissed*," said Jessie, accelerating away from a stoplight. Duncan sat beside her in the passenger seat of her Volkswagen. "She was all like, 'What have you *done* to him, Jessie?!' What a maniac."

"Yup, well, I'm her baby. And you tried to kill me."

He examined his face in the flip-down mirror. His nose looked as if it had been rhinoplastied by amateurs. His left eye was plum-colored, swollen halfway shut, and he seemed to be storing acorns in his mouth.

"For the last time, I'm sorry." She eased the car onto the school's inner drive. It was seven twenty on Friday morning. "And it was not an attempt on your life, either. When and if I try to kill you, I won't be using a maraca."

"That comforts me."

Duncan continued staring at his reflection. He lightly touched the cut on his nose, then cringed in pain.

"Stop doing that!" urged Jessie. "I can't stand it. It's like watching that video of the chimpanzee who smells his own butt and falls out of a tree. I mean, you *know* it's gonna stink. Stop touching it."

"It's just so weird. Look at me. I'm totally mauled. When have I ever been mauled? Never. I am not the type to stumble into a maiming or mauling. I can barely even see out of one eye. It's just . . . well, it's weird."

Jessie pulled into a parking spot.

"I'm happy to continue driving you to school while you're incapacitated," she said. "It was my flying maraca, after all. But stop with the self-obsession. You're like Tom Cruise in that movie where he gets disfigured by psycho Cameron Diaz."

"Wait, what am I like?"

"Oh, you know that movie. Tom Cruise is the rich du—"

"No, I mean am I like the butt-sniffing chimpanzee, or am I like Tom Cruise?"

"You're like a butt-sniffing Tom Cruise."

Duncan continued to eye himself in the mirror. "Dunno. But I am hideous."

They sat quietly for a moment, Jessie looking at Duncan look at himself.

"What am I going to tell people?" he eventually asked.

"That you're a flaming ninny who can't keep his balance, of course. What else would you tell people?"

"That's not really the image I'd like to project: flaming ninny."

"I'll follow your lead, Duncan, but if I were you, I'd go

with the truth. Just don't say too much—that's the key. Try to make your injuries seem mysterious. 'An accident in the garage,' you'll say. People will think you were being all toolsy and rugged. Was he repairing something? Was he welding? Was he hammering? They won't know, and you won't tell them. But they'll suspect it was something *dangerous.*"

"Right. Danger. That's Duncan Boone." He flipped up the mirror and turned to face Jess. "I really need to avoid Carly today. After my recent series of miscalculations, I can't face her with this, um . . . face. I just can't."

"Okay, dude. Normally I'd throw something at you for saying that, but we've seen where that can lead. So fine."

"You've gotta get my stuff from my locker, Jess. I'll try to keep a safe distance."

"And where exactly will you be, Elephant Man? Hiding your terrible secret in the shadows?"

"If I have to, yes."

"You're a pretty vain guy, Duncan. But whatever." They exited the car.

Jessie helped him maneuver slowly toward the school's main entrance, a boxy glass-and-steel atrium-thing that was apparently designed to make students feel like they were checking in to an Embassy Suites. Prepping us for later lives of business travel, Duncan often thought. As he walked through the school, students gaped at his puffy, discolored face. Given his limited vision, Duncan was only vaguely aware of the attention.

"Jess," he whispered, "it kinda sounds like people are murmuring. Am I being murmured about? I'd hate that."

"Be cool," she whispered back. "Of course you're being murmured about. You look like day-old vomit, dude. Just be cool. Keep your disfigured head up. 'A garage accident,' you'll say. And then say no more."

They climbed up the worn stairs that led to Duncan's locker, then plodded down the hallway. More gawking, more pointing, more murmuring from students. Jessie and Duncan stopped thirty feet short of his locker when they saw the hulking back of a football jersey: HURLEY 55.

"Oh, man," said Duncan. "Is that Perry Hurley? The Pear Bear?"

"Yup."

"At my locker? What's *that* about? He must've gotten himself lost on the way to the weight room."

"Dude is big," said Jessie. "And I don't think he's lost. I think he stopped by to mack on your girl, Duncan."

Perry Hurley, troglodytic three-sport all-conference athlete, was indeed talking to Carly. It was a game day for the football team, so Perry wore his Elm Forest Owls home jersey to school over a blue polo, his collar half popped. Carly leaned away from him, frowning, her arms folded across an embroidered peasant blouse. Perry rested an arm on Duncan's locker and bent down toward her. She backed up a little farther. He inched closer. She retreated. And so it went. Duncan listened from afar.

Perry: ". . . because you might actually have fun, that's why. Just come. It's not just a kegger. We'll have beer bongs and hookahs, too. Plus my buddy Buddha has a kick-ass indoor pool. So c'mon. Don't say no."

Carly: "Please don't take this the wrong way, Perry—Pear Bear—but I'd rather slit my wrists and drink my own blood."

"Point, Carly," said Jessie in a hushed voice. "That was well played."

"Told you she's a smart cookie."

"He's a total scuz."

More words passed between Perry and Carly before he at last backed off, hands raised in resignation, and said in an unnecessarily loud voice, "Suit yourself, Garfield. Have fun doing whatever it is you do."

He slapped two smaller jersey-wearing persons on the back, and the three began to walk away from Duncan's locker. As they did, an obviously frustrated Perry whacked several books out of the arms of a pasty freshman who'd drifted too close to him at exactly the wrong moment. Then he bumped the freshman aside with his forearm and loudly said, "Excuse me, dumbass." This seemed to amuse Perry's teammates greatly.

It did not seem to amuse Carly.

"Perry!" she snapped.

He stopped.

"Why would you do that?" Carly had rushed to the stunned freshman's aid, kneeling on the ground to pick up his textbooks.

"Kid got in my way," the linebacker said. "Total accident." Servile snickering from his teammates.

"You're such a fraud, Perry. And your groupies are worse." She glared. "You find the least-threatening person you can, and then you assault him. Why? Because I won't go with you to some lame-ass kegger on a lame cul-de-sac?"

"She said 'ass,'" Jessie whispered to Duncan. "Wow. She swears."

"Just little swears," Duncan clarified. "Not big ones."

Carly continued to berate Perry.

"You attacked another human being who one, you don't even know, and two, probably idolizes you. Because guys seem to idolize the dumbest, jockiest people they can find—and around here, there's no one dumber and more jocky than you." She crept closer to Perry, her eyes narrowing. "You're basically everything that's wrong with the whole popularity hierarchy, Perry. There always has to be some insecure loser at the top, just dumping their misery on everyone else."

Carly gripped the freshman's hand, which appeared to surprise the boy at least as much as having his books violently knocked to the floor. "Seriously," she continued, "what possible reason could you have for attacking him? You're messing the poor kid up, Perry. This—right now—is probably the most awkward moment of his life."

She turned toward the freshman.

"Is this awkward for you?" she asked softly.

He nodded.

"See!" yelled Carly. "He *is* messed up! And it's your fault, you gutless moron!"

Perry sheepishly offered, "I don't actually think you're doing the kid any favors right now, Car—"

"I'm treating him with respect."

She stood, vigorously shook her unopened organic cola, then sprayed it over Perry's crispy hair and clean jersey. He shrieked as if he were being set ablaze. A collective "ooooooh" arose from the students watching the confrontation.

"They're not booing," said Jessie mockingly. "They're hooting! Go Owls!"

Perry wiped cola from his face with his meaty hands and removed the jersey. He then eyed the freshman, who stood grinning behind Carly.

"You're dead," said Perry, pointing at him. "You are *d-e-a-* . . ."

"You will *not* touch him," said Carly firmly. "Or I will ruin you, Perry." She paused. "But please continue. We're all eager to know if you can spell 'dead.'"

After a bit more angry posing, the cola-soaked Pear Bear walked away, his friends trailing behind. Carly draped her arm around the freshman and walked him to her locker. She handed him a pamphlet and whispered something. He hurried off with a victorious grin.

"Oh, man!" Jessie excitedly declared. "You've *gotta* let that chick see your face, Duncan!"

"Wha—? Carly is the *last* person who needs to see my face when it's this misshapen."

"Nope," said Jessie. "She likes 'em that way."

With that, she launched Duncan toward Carly with an indelicate shove.

He stood no more than ten feet behind her, jittery and hesitant. He looked back toward Jessie with his good eye. She shoved him closer to his locker and, thus, to Carly Garfield, avenging angel.

"Oh my *Gawd*!" Carly exclaimed, lifting her head when she noticed Duncan. He braced himself for some derisive comment. Instead, this: "Oh, my. Oh, no. No, no, no . . ."

Carly gently brushed her hands across his face—the first instance of physical contact between them since a regrettable collision at home plate in a gym-class kickball game sophomore year. She drew him closer. His heart pounded.

"What happened?" Carly asked, her deep green eyes scanning his wounds.

"An accident in my gar—"

"He got beat up!" blurted Jessie, hopping behind Duncan. "Badly! Look at him! It's just awful!" She swept around Duncan and stood between him and Carly, speaking quickly. "Some thug jumped Duncan right after a band practice—you knew we were in a band, right? Duncan's a wicked good guitarist. Have you heard Duncan play? You should. He's great. Anyway, we're carrying the heavy instruments, no capacity to defend ourselves, and this thug—or maybe a collection of thugs, a whole herd of thugs. How many thugs were there, Duncan? Three? Four? What would you say?"

He looked at her quizzically and said "Uhhhm . . ." before Jessie continued.

"It happened so fast. Anyway, if it was just one guy doing the beating, which it might have been, he was *huge*. And he—or maybe they—totally kicked the crap out of poor Duncan. He's normally good-looking, you know, in a sensitive, artsy sort of way. But just not today. For obvious reasons. Anyway, Duncan tried to fight back, but he's so puny—look at him." Jessie flopped one of Duncan's long, thin arms. He scowled at her, thinking to himself that this was way more humiliation than he deserved.

But Carly radiated empathy. She cupped his bashed face in her startlingly soft hands.

"Oh, Duncan, you poor thing," she said, pouting. He was simultaneously flushed, panicked, and exhilarated. *She knows my name!* he thought. "What would make someone do something like this?" Carly asked.

"Oh, man," said Jessie. "Duncan has been terrorized for days. *Days*. It's just awful."

"But why?" asked Carly. "You're such a harmless boy." She gently twisted Duncan's face around to inspect his purple eye and swollen cheek.

"He is," insisted Jessie. "So harmless. Like a bunny. No, like an injured bunny—he's *that* harmless. But some people just abuse poor, defenseless little bunnies like Duncan. Makes them feel better about themselves, I guess."

"Bullies," said Carly. "Some people can't feel good about

themselves unless they're hurting someone else. It's just awful." She massaged Duncan's shoulder with her hand. "If I can help you with anything, Duncan—anything at all—just let me know. Poor thing."

"Actually," said Jessie, "if you could help get Duncan to first period, that would be so great. I was gonna do it, but I have to get way over to the east end of school, in the new wing. I'll be late if I help him get to class. But look at him." She extended her hand, as if presenting Duncan as a prize. "The boy's a victim. He definitely needs help. Can't see well enough to find his way. Terrible headaches. He can barely speak—I think his teeth are loose, maybe. He's just a wreck."

"Of *course* I'll help him," said Carly. "Poor fella." She sighed, removed his backpack from his shoulders, and squeezed his hand. "First a bird dookies on your folder, then life dookies on your face." She hugged him. Duncan hugged back.

Ecstatic, he winked at Jessie with the eye he could control.

The school day that followed was the most exhilarating seven hours that Duncan had ever experienced. Carly lugged his books from class to class, opened doors, scooted out chairs, led him by the hand. He considered asking her to prechew his food at lunch. And she might've done it, too—she was that nice. Somehow, Carly managed to dote on him without making him feel completely useless and feeble. She complimented him, joked with him, asked for his opinion. She also fed him a constant diet of TARTS-related information.

"Did you know that Elm Forest College does obesity test-ing with lab rats, Duncan?"

"No."

"They stuff them like piñatas."

"I had no idea."

"Isn't that cruel?"

"It's unspeakable."

"Exactly. You can get involved."

"I'll do anything."

He was like a cartoon boy following the perfumed vapor trail of a beautiful cartoon girl. Duncan drifted happily through-out the day. He agreed with basically everything she said—and she said a lot. By the end of the day, as she helped pack his book bag, he felt more smitten than he'd ever been.

"Thanks for all the help, Carly." He sagged against his locker. "I couldn't have gotten through the day without you."

She tilted her head and grinned, her warm, bright eyes scanning his face. "I had a very nice day, too, Duncan."

She hugged him, the book bag falling to the floor.

6

Friday afternoon, three fifty. The last of the buses had pulled away from school. Teachers marched to their cars under a row of halogen lights. A kid in an orange-and-brown Elm Forest mascot suit, sans Owl head, stood just off school property, smoking. Duncan sat on the hood of Jessie's Volkswagen, grinning as he sort of listened to an indie podcast. Mostly he was just reflecting on the astonishing magnificence of his day—the only day during which Carly had ever really acknowledged his existence in any meaningful, ongoing way.

Duncan removed his headphones. He idly ran his tongue over one of the small cuts in his mouth as he pulled his English journal from his backpack. He picked off a stray fleck of pigeon poo that he'd missed in the earlier cleaning and began to write.

ENTRY #10, SEPTEMBER 23

I won't disclose too much here, Mrs. Kindler, but
I will say this: today was pretty much the greatest
f*#@!ng day of my life. Sorry for the strong language
there. But it is my journal. And believe me, today was
so good, it was f*#@!ng good. Really. I won't say WHY
it was so good, though, because we're not quite there
yet in our relationship, Mrs. K.

But anyway, this was a pretty f*#@!ng amazing
day. (Just for reference, because I don't think you'll
actually be reading this entry for a while, today was
the day that I arrived at school with the black eye,
the fat lip, and the gaping wound across my nose.
And you said, "You're supposed to play the guitar
with your hands, Mr. Boone, not your face." And
everyone had a nice laugh at my expense. Good one,
Mrs. K. Take that comedy act to the riverboat casino.
Seriously.)

I haven't read any *Gatsby* since my last
prematurely terminated entry. And I'm not readin'
it tonight, either. Because tonight I celebrate the
greatest day of my life. Maybe tomorrow, though. So
if you're really only making your students hack away
at these journals so that we can demonstrate literary
insights that, for some reason, we haven't dared
share with the class, you can just skip ahead to entry

#11 right now. I promise that one's going to be piled high with thoughtful displays of the analytical tools that I've acquired in your class, Mrs. K. ☺ (That's me. Today. Because this is the greatest f*#@ ⌣

"Get the butt off my Jetta, Boone!" Jessie was jogging toward the car, with Stew lagging behind her. She sounded angry, but looked rather amused. "The butt!" she barked. "Off!"

Duncan did as he was told, hopping off the hood. He was still beaming. He quickly scribbled !ng day of my life. Later . . .) in the journal, closed it, and stuffed it back in his book bag. He kept smiling.

"Sorry, Duncan, but I'm kinda particular about which butts go on the hood of the car," Jessie said. "I have this fantasy where I lose my virginity on the hood, so I like to keep the surface pristine. Unblemished."

"Is this like a cop-pulls-you-over-on-a-lonely-highway sort of fantasy?" asked Stew. "Or more of a four-a.m.-outside-the-biker-bar fantasy?"

"I've revealed too much already," said Jessie, dismissively waving her hand. "But it's most definitely not a cop, just so you know."

"How was detention today?" asked Duncan.

"Detention is what it is, my man. Not everyone can do the time. They screw with your mind in there. Mr. Shah was humming today. *Humming*." Jessie loathed humming.

Duncan merely smiled.

"So," said Jessie, smirking, "I take it you had a pleasant day at school today. Anything you'd like to share with the band?"

Duncan became suddenly very self-aware. The grin flattened. After incurring Jessie's wrath on consecutive days for gushing and/or whining about Carly so extensively, he hoped to rein it in just a little. But, in fact, he was way past elated.

"It was . . . well, yeah. Good day, I guess."

"Missed you at lunch today, dude," said Stew.

"That was nice of Carly to escort you to *her* cafeteria table, though, you filthy dog," said Jessie, jabbing Duncan's arm.

"She unwrapped my Nutter Butters," he said.

"That all had to feel pretty surreal, eh? I mean, like, eight hours ago she thought you were . . . well, she never thought about you at all, not even once. And now you're like her little pet. An injured little purse dog that she can carry around. Like a Chihuahua, maybe. Or a Yorkie."

"Something like that," said Duncan. "Definitely a different sort of day for me. She must've told that story—your story, Jess—of the thug ambush a hundred times. 'Poor Duncan had no chance,' she'd say. And her friends would all say 'Aaaaaww.'" He paused. "Carly is just so . . ."

". . . unbelievably *stacked*," said Stew. "Like in a Lindsay Lohan–*Mean Girls* sort of way." Jessie jabbed him with her elbow.

". . . sincerely thoughtful," continued Duncan. "It was nice. And maybe it was a little surreal, too." He paused, working to contain his glee. "She sure is deep into that rodent-saving thing. She had these pictures of dissected rats in her locker."

"Gross, dude," said Stew. "I have pictures of Eva Longoria in my locker. I keep 'em behind my booster club calendar. It's a pretty sweet setup."

"Right," said Duncan. "Of course you do. Carly doesn't keep the rat pictures for personal gratification. She's just trying to save lab rats or something."

"Lame. Dissected rats? Not hot. Eva? Hot."

"So," said Jessie, again digging an elbow in Stew's ribs, "Carly just kept walking you to your classes today?" asked Jessie.

"Yup, every class," said Duncan. "All day."

"And did you play up the pain angle? 'Oooh, my face. It hurts sooo bad, Carly. Will you lick it?' Stuff like that?"

"No, I didn't solicit any licking. Not today. Maybe Monday. We'll see."

"Right, pace yourself," said Stew. "Asking a girl to lick you so early in a relationship is dicey. I know this."

Duncan doubted whether Stew, in fact, knew this. Not a player, Stew. Nice guy, excellent bassist, steady friend. Player? No. Lech? A little.

"How 'bout some big ups for your favorite drummer?" asked Jess. "I opened the door to the Carly Garfield home for wayward boys, y'know."

"Props to you," said Duncan, bowing just slightly. "It was a bold lie. That could've gone badly."

"Oh, *bah*!" she said. Jessie opened the Volkswagen and hopped behind the wheel. "I can't believe you didn't ask me to wreck your face years ago, dude. That girl has a total victim complex. She's a whale-saver. A tree hugger. No, she's not just hugging trees—she's doing even more graphic things to trees. That girl is looking for things to protect. If you want her to be interested in you, then you have to appear endangered. Like that tiny freshman this morning."

"Or like me, with my face bashed in."

"Precisely."

They squealed out of the lot.

"Where to?" asked Jessie. "Casa del Boone? We can graze on Oreos and Diet Squirt, then jam awhile, and then go to the football game—I'm thinking our friend the Pear Bear has some aggression to release on unsuspecting ball carriers. Or we could just graze, jam, then go to Duncan's basement for some no-life club."

No-life club meant PlayStation, MP3s, and further grazing.

"I vote no-life," said Stew.

"Seconded," said Duncan.

"That was democratic of us," said Jess.

"My house it is," said Duncan.

Jessie wove through after-school traffic with reckless ease, pounding her hands on the fur-covered steering wheel in time to the car's stereo. Stew bobbed his head, pounded the dashboard, and sang badly. He was not allowed to sing with Fat Barbie. He could mouth words, but never sing.

Duncan spent the short ride home sitting in the backseat thinking—on the verge of worry, actually. He considered Jessie's comment: "You have to appear endangered." She'd recognized this fact immediately, almost intuitively. The simplest way to get Carly's attention was clearly to play on her endless reserve of compassion. It didn't seem reasonable to go to school with fresh injuries every day, though. Which meant that he had a very narrow window of time in which to impress Carly with something other than the fact that he'd been recently victimized. (Which, of course, he hadn't been. Not really.) And his various injuries were probably going to improve over the weekend when he'd have no opportunity to see Carly. For the time being, he needed the black eye and the various lacerations—it was the essence of his victim-ness, which was the essence of his appeal to his do-gooder, rodent-saving dream girl. If he showed up at school on Monday in good health, the consequences were dire: no more walks to class with Carly; no more lunches with Carly; no more fawning from Carly, period.

They pulled into Duncan's driveway, exited the car, and walked toward the front door. Jess and Stew were engaged in a game in which they attempted to have a semirational conversation using only song titles; this quickly degenerated into a Smiths versus Fall Out Boy showdown. Duncan threw open the screen door, yelled hello to whoever might be listening, and headed for the kitchen. Jessie helped herself to the Oreos and soda. Talia skipped through, inquired about Duncan's face, then left. Duncan's mother rushed in and snatched her keys from a wall hook near the fridge. She gave Jessie a sharp look, which was ignored—Jessie being lost in the bliss of sugar and saturated fat—and then addressed her son.

"How was school today, dear? Still feeding at the trough of self-pity?"

"No, Mom. All better now. How was your day?"

"Principal Donovan is the lowest form of amoebic scu—" She stopped, smiled coyly, and then said, "It was delightful.

Another perfect day. Nothing to report. Need anything from the store, honey?"

"You're low on Oreos, Mrs. Boone," said Jessie.

"I'm glad you feel so welcome here, Jessica."

"Okay, Mrs. Boone," she said through a mouthful of cookie. "I'll give you one 'Jessica' since I played a small role in breaking your son's head. But that's it. Anyway, you're low on Oreos."

"Noted," said Duncan's mom as she left.

Duncan sat pensively for a moment while Jessie and Stew foraged in the walk-in pantry. He felt his swollen eye, then his lip and nose.

"So," he said, "what happens when my face heals?"

"Then you go back to being ugly for all the usual reasons," said Stew.

"No, I mean . . . well, yeah, that, sure. But what I mean is—"

"—what happens with Carly," said Jessie. She bit into a stack of cheese-flavored chips.

"Exactly. I won't look like this for long. I'll recuperate. And then she'll forget about me again."

"But you've got a foot in the door, dude," said Stew.

"His foot's in a door marked 'Helpless Victims,' though," said Jess.

"Yup," agreed Duncan. "Once my face heals, she's indifferent to me."

"Join that TARTS thing," said Stew. "I mean, unless they're too political. I don't wanna be in a band that's totally political.

We're not, like, flower children. Our message is loud and simple: rock, motherf—"

"Dude! My little sister is giving her Barbie a makeover in the next room."

"Right. Our message is this: rock, people of the western suburbs."

"Anyway, I did join TARTS. Sort of. I filled out the form on the back of a pamphlet. I might send it in."

"But you need to stay beaten up," said Jess.

"Yeah, that's what I'm thinking. At least for now."

"Easy enough," said Stew. "The best way to provoke violent assaults is to keep pissing off Jess. She'll give you beat-downs as needed."

"Right," said Duncan. "Because that's so enjoyable."

"You need a different assailant," said Jessie, a spray of orange crumbs flying from her mouth. "I'm not crossing Carly, man. That girl fights back. Ask Hurley."

"But you agree that I *do* need an assailant, right?" asked Duncan. "I need a thug."

Jessie and Stew stared at him for a long, silent moment.

"It's hard to tell if you're kidding, Duncan, because your face is so bashed up," said Jessie. "You *are* kidding, right?"

"No." He returned the stare. "At least I don't think I'm kidding."

"You actually *want* to get the crap kicked out of you?" asked Jessie. "Repeatedly? To impress the only girl on earth who might actually be impressed by this?"

"I think I do. I mean, it would be nice if I didn't actually have to suffer any more facial injuries."

"But you'd accept, say, a broken femur?" asked Jess. "Or a lacerated spleen? A ruptured appendix? Broken fingers?"

"No, not the fingers. Can't play guitar with broken fingers."

"Oh, yeah," said Stew. "We might have to cancel a gig. Or maybe the entire Asian tour. That'd sure suck."

"Anyway, I don't actually want to get *hurt*. But we laid the groundwork for me being terrorized by a thug, and Carly ate it up. This victim thing is my in with her."

"And so you're thinking you need to provoke some scary thug?" said Jessie. "Maybe get him to chase you around the lunchroom or something? Hmm. That's some crazy-in-love desperation right there, Duncan."

"You said to take radical action."

"That I did. But what I really meant was, y'know . . . try *talking* to the girl. Write her a note, maybe. Or go the secret admirer route. I didn't mean that you should risk injury."

"Well, I don't actually want to get hurt. I'm not that self-destructive—it's my tragic weakness as a musician. Well, that and not being able to master any Satriani arpeggios."

"So what are you thinking?" Jessie asked.

Duncan fidgeted for a few seconds. He tapped his foot against the kitchen floor and rubbed his temples, then looked up.

"I'd like to hire a bully," he said.

Jessie and Stew stared again. Jess placed the chip bag on the counter and wiped her hands.

"Okay. Let's have a look at the yearbook."

7

They sat perusing the glossy pages of yearbooks, suggesting potential goons who might be willing to assault him for profit. Names were written on a kitchen chalkboard, then erased, then new names proposed. Some were deemed too unattainable given their position in the social strata (like Perry); others were judged too inadvisable because they were criminally unhinged (like Erik "the Yeti" Slutzer). Ultimately, all EFTHS goons presented the same insurmountable problem: despite their goonishness, they had friends. All of them. Eventually, they were likely going to discuss Duncan's plan with these friends. And if word leaked that Duncan tried to recruit a bully to fake-attack him so that he could elicit sympathy from Carly Garfield, that would obviously doom his chances with her. So if Duncan was going to choreograph any acts of bullying, *no one* could find out. This was imperative.

And it seemed impossible. After twenty minutes spent vetting various candidates—and ruling all of them out—they were interrupted by Duncan's father, an ample man dressed in a red Izod shirt and dark brown Dockers.

"'Lo," he said, whistling.

"Evenin', Mr. Boone," chirped Jessie. "Did you see what I did to your son's face?"

"Mmm-hmm," said Mr. Boone. He scanned the pantry shelves. "No Oreos?"

"Mom's at the store," said Duncan.

"Mmm." He turned, opened the fridge, and withdrew a package of gray sausages, then strolled outside.

"Your dad is complex," said Stew.

"A serious thinker," agreed Duncan. "He's what Mrs. Kindler would call 'an archetype.'" Duncan ran his hands through his hair, then sighed. "So hiring a thug is hopeless, I guess."

"Hopeless?" said Jessie. "No. But there are many risks, and the only reward is that your dream girl will think you're a doofus."

"She loves doofuses."

"We know that she loves *saving* them. We do not know that she loves *them*."

"Right," said Duncan. "But Carly never said a word to me until I was oozing blood, and now she can't get enough of me. That ends if there are no more assaults. It'd be nice just to stage something. Nothing huge—nothing that leaves me dismembered. I just need a little victimization."

"If you're asking me to attack you again, the answer is still no," said Jessie, grinning.

"And I'm totally nonviolent," said Stew.

Talia raced through the kitchen noisily. A yellow Nerf bullet followed her, just missing her feet as she zigzagged between chairs. Emily entered the room breathless, a purple-and-orange semiautomatic Nerf gun in her right hand. She paused, staring at Duncan.

"Oh, sweet!" she said, huffing. "It's true! You really do look awful! It couldn't happen to a bigger turd!" Emily popped off two Nerf bullets at Duncan. He blocked one with his hand, but the other clipped his left ear. Emily scurried off.

"Evil gnome!" yelled Duncan.

"She's a charmer," said Jessie.

"You two share an affinity for hitting me with stuff."

"She's in Talia's class?" asked Stew. "Really? She seems too big."

"No, she goes to Reagan Math and Science. Private school brat. She gets picked up by a bus full of . . ."

"Duh!" said Jessie, standing. "Another school."

Duncan and Stew stared at her with blank faces.

"We're looking for Duncan's bully in the wrong school," she said. "We could find someone at Maple North, maybe. If it's too risky to use one of our fellow Owls, then we'll get a Maple North Viking. It's perfect."

"We don't know any thuggy Maple students, do we?" asked Stew.

"Nope," said Jessie. "But there must be some. We'll scout them in the visitors section tonight."

"Because you think that all the Maple North thugs attend the away football games?" Duncan asked.

"No, but we could still poke around a little, compile names, ask who the thugs are."

"How weird is *that*?" said Duncan.

"So you'd rather forgo this pretend-to-be-bullied ruse," snapped Jessie, "in favor of the old approach: stalking Carly and always doing something idiotic when you're around her?"

Duncan drummed on the kitchen table for a moment.

"Okay," he said. "We talk to Vikings."

They returned to EFTHS, where Duncan discovered that he very much enjoyed the anonymity of the visiting team's sideline. The threshold for embarrassing oneself was extremely high—especially when those around you were being led in cheers by a shirtless ax-wielding kid in plastic horns and a Viking beard. Jessie, pretending to represent the Elm Forest student newspaper, the *Owl's Nest*, roamed the sidelines badgering Maple North students, ostensibly for a "Know your rivals" feature. Stew took notes. It had been decided that Duncan's bruises made him a liability in a face-to-face interview. Neither Jess nor Stew had any actual affiliation with the school paper, although Jessie had once written a strongly worded letter to the editor (unpublished) excoriating them for recommending a Ryan Cabrera song as prom theme. She peppered Maple North students with questions like "Who's the hottest guy in school?" (no clear winner) and "Who's your creepiest teacher?" (by an overwhelming margin, a History teacher named Dr. Ween) and "Do you know where

Vikings came from?" (most said Scandinavia, though two said "Viking Land"). The only question that really meant anything to the questioners, however, was "Who's the toughest kid in school?"

After a thorough canvassing of Viking fans, Jessie sat on an empty patch of bleacher near Duncan. "We've established the identity of the alpha-bully at Maple North," she declared.

"And he is . . . ," said Duncan with mock anxiousness.

"A boy named Sloth."

"Is he slow-moving?" asked Duncan.

"What?" asked Jessie.

"Sloths are slow. It's their diet. All leaves."

"No," said Jessie. "Doesn't sound like he's a leaf-eater. As I understand it, he's just furry."

"Thus, Sloth," said Stew.

"A nickname," Jessie said. "Real name, Ted Gleeman. He's a fifth-year senior, rumored to be as old as twenty. Possibly psychotic. Regarded by most as totally unapproachable."

"Totally?"

"Well, no one approaches him at school," said Jessie. "And he's rarely called upon in class. An assistant dean told me—off the record—that the faculty is determined to see Sloth graduate. He scares them." She paused. "So we'll confront him away from school grounds. Tomorrow. I have a lead on his residence."

"That's some fine journalism," said Duncan.

"I have a way with people," she said. "I'm a bubbly gal when you get right down to it."

Duncan shifted uncomfortably.

"Don't worry," said Jessie flatly. "I make the initial contact. I'm just an unthreatening girl. What's the worst that can happen?"

"He crushes your skull, then eats your entrails," said Stew.

"You forget my way with people," she said.

A simple Web search back at Duncan's confirmed Jessie's lead: "T. Gleeman" indeed lived at the Mallard Brooke apartment complex in Maple Grove. On Saturday morning, after a late night of no-life, Duncan, Stew, and Jessie hopped back in her car, bought coffees, and staked out Mallard Brooke Apartment 312. It was located in a recently annexed section of Maple Grove, near a cluster of industrial buildings. They sat anxiously in the late-morning light, sipping.

"So we'll just observe Sloth," Duncan said. "In his natural habitat. If we don't think he can help, we move on."

"To what?" asked Stew.

"There's always a plan B."

"I'm guessing plan B involves Carly tied up in the back of a rented van," said Jessie.

Duncan laughed. "Don't be ridiculous," he said. "I'm not old enough to rent a van." He slid down low in the front seat and stuck his feet outside the window.

"All feet must be inside the car, please," said Jessie.

"Why, do you have sexual fantasies that involve the passenger-side front window?"

She flicked Duncan's ear with her finger. "No, I do not. But I've seen lots of films where cops go on stakeouts, and I've never once seen a fictional detective sit with his feet out the window. It's not done."

"Um . . . we're not cops." Duncan removed the plastic lid of his coffee and swirled it with his index finger. "I was just trying to be casual in case anyone noticed us."

"Like who?" asked Stew. "The Mallard Brooke security force? Not likely."

Duncan looked up to the apartment in which he believed Sloth resided. Sunlight glinted off the tiny windows and the brown metal balcony. A gray stairwell was strewn with discarded beer cans and fast-food bags. The shrubs were overgrown. The grass was beige.

"The Gleeman family doesn't seem to be doing well," he said.

"This place has perks," said Jess. "See, there's a pool."

She pointed toward a small rectangular pit that was covered by a layer of dead leaves. A lifeguard's chair was on its side. The pool was surrounded by a padlocked fence.

"If I ever do have that sex on my hood, get pregnant, drop out of school, and get kicked out of my house, I'm totally moving in here."

They sat in the Mallard Brooke lot until nearly noon, surveying the infrastructure. No one bothered them. In fact, very few residents or visitors appeared.

"We should leave," Duncan eventually said. "This is insane."

"Oh, c'mon," said Jessie. "I thought you were *in love*." She made exaggerated smooching sounds in Duncan's direction.

"I'm getting uneasy," he said. "I'm also getting hungry. But mostly uneasy."

"About what? About this incredibly twisted, desperate plot to deceive the girl of your dreams through an unnecessarily complicated act of trickery? One that can't possibly end with her happy and you guiltless, by the way."

"No, no. I'm cool with that."

"Oh, good. I thought you were getting all weenie on me."

"No, I'm uneasy about Sloth." Duncan crumpled his empty cup.

"Let's suppose we eventually do see a large, young, furry dude. What then?" He shifted in his seat. "I'm just uneasy."

"I've got your back," said Jess.

"No offense, since you've recently kicked my ass, but I'd feel better if I had more backup than a tiny punk rock girl and a nonviolent bassist." Duncan turned to face Stew, who was sprawled across the backseat. "Bassists are supposed to be notorious brawlers, by the way."

"I took tae kwon do for six months," he answered.

"We were seven," said Duncan.

"I broke a board with my elbow." Stew made a slow chopping motion in Duncan's direction.

"Can we please just get some lunch?" Duncan pleaded. "We can come ba—"

A gray-green Chevy screeched into a parking spot on the opposite side of the lot. A name appeared across the rear window in Old English script:

𝕾𝕷𝕺𝕿𝕳

Stew bolted upright.

"Hmm," said Duncan.

"Looky!" said Jessie. She grinned at Duncan. "I'm gonna go introduce myself!"

Duncan gripped her arm before she could open the door.

"To who?" he asked. "The driver of that car? We don't know that's Sloth just because it says 'Sloth' on the window. That could be a family member—his mom borrowing the car, maybe. Or it could be . . ."

". . . a different Sloth altogether?" said Jess sardonically. "You're right, Duncan. That could be any old Sloth."

"Well, let's just wait a second," Duncan said. "There's no sense getting out and walking over there until we know that it's . . ."

An astonishingly hairy person wearing a red flannel shirt emerged from the car. He seemed to roll out. He scratched his prominent gut and shrugged his shoulders as he stood beside the open door. His arms angled away from his massive chest, as if ready to draw guns. Or bring down a foal and drag it to his cave.

"Oh," said Duncan.

"That's our boy," said Stew.

Jessie wrenched free and opened the driver's-side door. She began walking quickly toward the Chevy. Duncan and Stew soon followed. Duncan felt a jolt of fear as Sloth beheld them for the first time. His unkempt beard began high up on his cheeks and continued down his neck. He wore a backwards Cubs cap and scuffed work boots.

"Hey there!" shouted Jess, sounding uncharacteristically perky. Sloth twitched, saying nothing. "You don't happen to go to North, do you?"

Slowly, almost robotically, Sloth's lips began to move. "Yee-aay-ah," he grumbled. His eyes narrowed.

"So you're Sloth, then? Like it says on the window. Do you prefer Sloth or—"

"Sloth'll do," he muttered.

"Great," said Jessie. An uncomfortable pause followed. "So," she continued, "we have a favor to ask. Actually, it's more of an arrangement to discuss." She stepped aside and swept her arm out toward Duncan. "Sloth, meet Duncan. Duncan, meet Sloth."

Sloth spit a loogie onto the asphalt. "Hey," he said.

"Hi!" said Duncan, sounding squeaky and nervous. "Hi," he said again in a deliberately lower-than-usual tone. "Hi," he repeated, finding his normal voice.

"So, Duncan?" said Jessie, urging him to make his pitch.

"Right," he said. "My friends and I have become familiar with your reputation. It's impressive." Sloth's face was totally still. Duncan reasoned that it couldn't be easy to identify any emotions, no matter how strongly felt they were, in someone so scary.

"My reputation," Sloth repeated.

"Yes," Duncan said. "As your school's preeminent tough guy. Um . . . tough person. Person of toughness."

Sloth simply stared. He was several inches taller than Duncan, and at least a foot wider.

"Tough," said Sloth, yawning.

"Yes," said Duncan. "That's the opinion of your class-mates. We took a poll."

"So you don't go to North?" Sloth asked.

"Nope," said Stew. "But we hear it's nice. Except for that Dr. Ween."

"Yeah, he's a weirdo," said Sloth, nodding.

"Anyway," said Duncan, his voice wavering, "we've heard a lot about you."

Sloth took a step forward, causing Duncan to recoil. Sloth looked at him curiously, then reopened his car door, removing a backpack.

"Is there somethin' you need, Duncan?" Sloth asked. He pointed at Duncan's battered face. "If you want someone to protect you, you've got—"

"Oh no!" said Jessie. "He doesn't need protection. He needs another beat-down."

"Well," said Duncan, "not a *real* beat-down, but a sort of choreographed beat-down that doesn't injure me so much as make me seem helpless and weak and, um . . . sad."

Sloth stared.

"That's messed up," he said.

"Yeah, well, I can see why you might think that," said Duncan. "It is kind of messed up. You're absolutely right." He began to sweat.

"Duncan is in a unique situation," said Jessie. "He sort of needs to get bullied in order to get this chick he likes to pay attention to him."

"Is she hot?" asked Sloth.

"Kinda hot, I guess," said Jessie, sneering. "If you're into—"

"She is undeniably hot, yes," said Stew. "Devastatingly, breathtakingly, mind-bendingly hot. Yes."

"What kinda hot chick is into beat-up dudes?" asked Sloth. "That's sick."

"I'm with you, brothah!" yelled Jessie, throwing her hands up.

"An incredibly sympathetic, compassionate girl," said Duncan. "That's what kind."

"And she's hot?" asked Sloth.

"Oh, sorta," said Jess, "if you can overlook—"

"*Yes,*" said Duncan. "Any reasonable heterosexual would tell you she's hot, yes. And fantastically nice. Like a kitten." He paused. "Does it matter that she's hot?"

"Nope," said Sloth, yawning again. "That just sounds messed up."

"Yeah, well, on the surface, maybe," agreed Duncan. "I'm not here to argue that. But could you still help? I'd pay you. Or I'd write a paper for you."

"Threaten you?" asked Sloth.

"Yup," said Duncan.

"'Fraid not," said Sloth. He began to walk slowly toward the stairwell. "You guys wanna come up? I've got leftover squash curry from this Thai place."

Duncan, Stew, and Jessie stared at one another, confused.

"Well, we don't want to disturb your family."

"I live alone," said Sloth, trundling off.

Duncan shuddered. Sloth lures us into his lair, he thought. Then he carves us up and leaves our bones at the bottom of the pool. Then he . . .

Jessie and Stew were already on Sloth's heels, following. Duncan shuddered again, then ran to catch up.

"You live *alone*?" Jess asked. "How cool."

"Not very," said Sloth. "I work third shift, which sucks. I get home from school, go to bed, get up at ten, go to work, then to school again."

"Eek," she said.

"I'm too busy to threaten you, Duncan. Sorry. And I'm not really the threatening type anyway." He fished in his pocket for his keys.

"But just about every North student—and more than one faculty member—agreed that you were the scariest guy in school," said Jessie.

"A convenient reputation," said Sloth. "I don't discourage it." He yawned again.

"So you really won't attack me?" asked Duncan.

"Sorry."

"Really, I'm willing to take on homework," offered Duncan. "I can write a pretty mean comparative essay."

"Me, too," said Sloth.

Duncan wilted.

Sloth opened the door to his apartment. The decor was tasteful and bright. Framed pictures of family members sat on end tables. "Leave your shoes by the door, please."

8

"Question: Could that have possibly been a *bigger* waste of my time?" Duncan leaned his head against the Volkswagen's window while Jessie drove. "Answer: No."

"Oh, stop," said Jess. "We met a pretty cool guy."

"We met a guy who looks like serial killer but is, in fact, a Boy Scout. And more importantly, he's a Boy Scout who's too busy—and too nice—to help me."

"We made a friend and had some day-old curry. Tasty day-old curry, I might add. And we learned a lesson."

"What's that?"

"That you can't judge a book by its cover." Jessie sighed contentedly.

"Or a sloth by its fur," said Stew. "Or something."

"I already learned that one," said Duncan. "In kindergarten. Everyone learned it in kindergarten." Duncan's head fell into his hands.

"So you didn't prejudge Sloth as a thug just because he was huge, allegedly crazy, and his name was *Sloth*?" asked Jessie.

"Of course I did. But I knew I *shouldn't* prejudge him. Fear just took over. So I really didn't learn anything—at best, a lesson that I didn't need was reinforced." Duncan lifted his head and looked toward Jessie. "The only thing I really learned today is this: I'm screwed. Utterly screwed."

"Just chill. First of all, Sloth was only our first attempt to find you a thug. Don't give up hope—there are plenty of nasty dudes out there just waiting for us to solicit them. And secondly, your face still looks like total crap, so Carly isn't going to just forget about this bullying stuff by Monday morning."

"The puffiness is already going away," said Duncan. He poked at his purplish eyelids and cheek. "See, this would have really hurt yesterday. I'm getting better. Which sucks."

Jess pulled the car into Duncan's driveway.

"And it's only Saturday afternoon," he added. "So I'll be healing for another forty hours or so before Carly sees me."

"Well, whatever you do, dude, don't ice yourself. There's no way that eye's gonna look human again by Monday morning."

"Would you still walk a guy to class if he had this eye?"

"Duncan, I can't imagine *what* condition a guy would have to be in for Jessie Panger to walk him to class and carry his stuff. He'd probably have to be blind, armless, not unattractive, and a pretty big fan of eighties hardcore. A black eye wouldn't really inspire me. I can't relate to Carly, dude."

"Right. Of course. I was a fool to ask."

"Practice tonight, then reconvene no-life club?" asked Stew.

"I have a vicious God of War addiction to feed," said Jess.

"Sure thing," said Duncan. He sighed.

Jessie patted his back (hard, like a golfer pats another golfer). "Buck up, buddy," she said. "Or use this period of personal misery to craft achingly sweet, emotive rock anthems. Whatever."

Duncan moped out of the car and Jess squealed off. He retreated to his room to catch up on homework. After reading not quite a full page of *Gatsby*, he realized he'd absorbed nothing. Duncan attempted to reread the passage, but instead fell asleep. The book fell to the floor. Hours passed.

He awoke to a sharp rap at his bedroom door, then his mom's voice: "Duncan, are you in there? Hon?"

"Mmmblugh," he managed.

"Your father and I are taking Talia and Emily out for dinner," she said through the door. "We're either doing Chuck E. Cheese or Olive Garden. Do either of those sound good?"

Duncan clutched his pillow. "Is death an option?" he said.

"It's a metaphysical certainty, honey," replied his mom. "But not for dinner. Tonight we decide between pizza and pasta. Are you coming with?"

"And be trapped with that slug-eater Emily? No chance, Mom."

"Suit yourself, sweetie. Can we bring you anything?"

"Pepperoni if you go pizza. Chicken marsala if you go Italian."

"You're a predictable boy, honey."

"You have no idea, Mom."

He listened to his mom's footsteps down the hall, then the stairs. She jingled her keys, called the girls, then slammed the front door shut. Duncan reached for his phone to check the time. 6:58. He called Jess. She answered quickly.

"Hey," she said.

"Hey," he said sleepily. "C'mon over. Practice begineth."

"Right, cool. We're really going to play, right? We're not just arguing set lists or arcane band philosophy or dissecting the subtleties of your latest eye contact with Carly?"

"No, just practice, sans bassist." He yawned. "But if you would just do what I say, when I say it, there'd be no arguments."

"A band can't be a dictatorship, dude."

"If only. That's really the problem with bands. I may have to launch the solo career."

"You'd be lost without me, dude. Like Mick without Keith. You ever hear one of those Mick Jagger solo efforts? Not pretty."

"Right. But I bet that band works so well because Keith does what he's told. Just collect Stew and come over," Duncan said.

Click.

He snatched his math textbook and a notebook from his desk, then ambled downstairs to snack and read. But first he examined himself in the mirror of the downstairs bathroom. "Approximately eight percent less puffy," he said of his eye. "Dang." Duncan sulked as he entered the kitchen. He blindly grabbed a bag of chips from the pantry, then pulled himself up onto the kitchen counter and threw open the book. He really had zero interest in homework, complex problem sets, or any aspect of his education. He needed to wallow. And vent. And wallow again. He yawned, then stuffed a handful of chips into his mouth. Then he closed the book, tossed it aside, and descended into the basement.

He grabbed an acoustic guitar and strummed lightly. Distracted and dejected, he threw himself down onto the couch to brood. Jessie soon hopped downstairs.

"What's the matter, rocker?" she said.

"Oh, hey," said Duncan. "Feel free to let yourself in." He sat up. "No Stew?"

"Sleeping. His mom didn't seem to want me to wake him, either. I don't think she trusts me. What is this effect I have on moms, anyway?"

"They sense wickedness," said Duncan. He stood and sighed. "Should we go practice?"

"But you seem so glum."

"You're not the sit-and-listen type of girl, remember? So let's just jam. I'll work through my teenage angst-crap musically."

"Well, luckily this situation does not call for me to sit and listen, Duncan—which is not really my thing, as we've discussed—because I know what's wrong with you. It's rat-girl."

"She's not just a rat-girl. She's protecting all the rodents of the world. There are, like, over a thousand different kinds—

and not just mice and rats. That's what the big pharmaceutical companies and their lobbyists *want* you to think. Or at least that's what Carly wants me to think the pharmaceutical companies want me to think. Anyway, squirrels are rodents, for example. So are marmots, beavers, prairie dogs, porcupines, muskrats, woodchucks, and a lot of other things I've forgotten. And Carly loves them all—it's sweet, really."

"You're telling me that labs are performing experiments on beavers?"

"Maybe. I don't know. I'll ask. But the point is that they *could* be experimenting on beavers, because no one's protecting them."

"Except Carly and her beaver club."

"Let's not call them that."

Jessie tucked her legs underneath her, then wrapped a quilt around her shoulders.

"In any case, I'm willing to allow some discussion about how to proceed with you and Carly if we can't find you a bully."

"There is no me and Carly without a bully. The bully is the flint to ignite the fire that *is* me and Carly. Without the flint, no sparks. Without the sparks, no big roaring inferno of—"

"—of Duncan and beaver-girl. I get it."

Duncan glared at her. "Because you've been trying to help me—which I appreciate—I'm gonna let the beaver talk go."

"You're in no position to threaten me, dude," said Jess, grinning.

"So we were going to discuss my wooing Carly."

"Right," said Jess, shifting slightly. "You know, we do have a few other thug names from our systematic sampling of Maple North students. We could try 'em."

"Sloth was their king, though. Those North kids are soft. And I couldn't endure another stakeout."

"Me either, really." She thought for a moment. "Ooh, here's an idea: we'll call administrators at other high schools— not just North—and pretend to be military recruiters. Then we ask for the names of the most disruptive and troubled kids. I'd bet we'll get good leads."

"Don't you think there might be something illegal about pretending to be military recruiters? Like, *seriously* illegal. Like they throw you in a small cage in a secret island prison and put electrodes on our shaved heads."

"Yeah, maybe," Jess said, sighing. "We could go to Tacos de Paco downtown and look for bullies. It's been my experience that thug-looking guys really enjoy the cheap burritos."

"Dude, all men are drawn to burritos. They call to us. *'¡Cómame, amigos!'* they say. And we obey them. They are not simply for thugs."

"Oohhhh-kay." She raised an eyebrow.

"Mrs. Kindler would call that anthropomorphizing," Duncan said. "The talking burritos."

"Right. So we don't look for bullies at the burrito place. Fine. There must be other ways to find them." Jess frowned, thinking hard. "How 'bout we dress Stew up as some kind of übergeek—the thick glasses, the button-down oxford—and we

use him as bait. Maybe take him to a mall and wait for someone to antagonize him. Then, when they do, you and I swoop
in and offer to hire them."

"Number one, that's a lot to ask of Stew. Number two—
and this is really the deal-breaker—if these mall thugs somehow managed to hurt Stew before we could get there, Carly
would start lavishing attention on *him*. We can't have that. It
would lead to friction, mistrust, and general band discord." He
tapped his fingertips together. "Let's face it: things are hopeless."

"You could just try being honest with Carly," Jessie said.
"Maybe express what you're actually feeling."

Duncan chuckled. "You're high, Jess. It's waaaaaay too
early in the relationship for honesty. Once you've played the
honesty card, it's over. There are no more cards to play."

"So honesty is only to be attempted after you're completely out of BS? Is that how it works? Hmm. Interesting."

"Kinda. At least in this case. I was hoping to save honesty
for, like, last week of senior year. Unless Carly and I were ever
drunk together, which seems even less likely than our dating."

Jessie fumbled with the collection of remotes hidden in
various chair crevices. She turned on the TV, then the game
system, then grabbed a controller. She and Duncan continued
discussing his bully/Carly options while she gamed. Eventually, they began to hear upstairs noises: keys, the front door,
indecipherable conversation, giggly kids.

"Food's here," said Duncan. "Finally."

Jessie grunted at the TV, swerving to duck some pixelated missile. Duncan leapt up the stairs.

"Hey, Mom," he said. "Jess is over. She's gaming. Where's dinner?"

"Missed you, too, son," said his smiling father, angling past him on his way to the fridge.

"There are several pizza slices in a Styrofoam container," said Duncan's mom. "The wait at Olive Garden was ninety minutes. We went to Chuck E."

"I won a plastic butterfly!" said Talia, hopping. "It lights up!" She squeezed it. It lit up.

"Emily won sparkly stickers and Silly Putty!" Talia said. Emily stretched the Silly Putty and grinned.

"Fantastic," said Duncan. "That's great news, T. Now, where's the pizza?"

Emily handed him a Styrofoam box. Duncan looked toward his mom.

"You let the troll handle the food?" he asked incredulously.

"It was in the backseat," said his mom, flipping through mail.

"And the troll was also in the backseat with the pizza, doing who-knows-what?"

Talia squeezed her butterfly. "Stop calling my friend a troll!" she said.

"Duncan, stop calling your sister's friend a troll," said his dad. The troll smiled quietly, gripping the pizza.

"Mom," he said, "did the food really ride with Emily? Really? The whole time?"

"I guess so, honey. But I'm sure the pizza's fine. Emily is a lovely girl." She nudged him with the pizza box.

"Have some," Emily said, grinning wider. "If you're feeling lucky." She snickered.

Duncan grabbed a bag of chips and went downstairs. "I'm really not," he said. "Not at all."

9

The remaining hours of the weekend passed uneventfully. Fat Barbie's Saturday practice consisted of Duncan picking at the acoustic guitar while Jessie made fighting noises—"AAY-YAH!" and "BWAP!" and "KEE-YOW!"—in response to video games. On Sunday it drizzled. Duncan spent the day completing problem sets, writing Spanish paragraphs, reading more *Gatsby*, then journaling about it as he'd promised Mrs. Kindler in his previous entry. At regular intervals, he checked on the size and coloration of his assorted facial injuries. Every time he did this, his reaction was the same: Oh, not good. Getting smaller. Crap.

Jessie drove him to school on Monday, although by then he was seeing just fine out of his still-purplish but far less swollen left eye. The cut on his nose no longer oozed anything. His mouth no longer ached. Things were correcting and realigning.

"Great to see you doing better, Duncan," said Carly. She smiled.

Duncan noticed the array of TARTS buttons on the long strap of her purse. Nice that she remembers my name, he thought. Incredibly bad that she noticed improvement.

"Oh, things still hurt. A lot." He grimaced in fake-pain as he swung his backpack off his shoulder. "Ohwwoo," he added for emphasis. "I'm still a little freaked about getting jumped by tha—"

"See ya, Duncan," she said, slamming shut her locker. "I've got a meeting. Big TARTS rally. Busy, busy. Sooo exciting!" She raced off.

Duncan watched her float down the hall.

And so it ends, he thought. No walking me to class today. No sympathy caressing. No invitation to lunch. No attention, period. He sighed. Soon it'll be "Dalton" again. And then I'm back to repelling her. And then . . . poof. Nothing. Nada. The empty set.

He opened his locker and fussed with its contents absentmindedly. Minutes before first period, Stew and Jessie ambled by.

"Where's your girl?" Stew asked.

"She's busy being not anywhere near me," Duncan answered.

"Have you seen her yet?" asked Jessie.

"There were pleasantries. Incredibly brief. Like you'd exchange with a clerk at Kwik Mart. Nothing of substance. It's over."

"No offense, dude, but 'over' implies that it started, which it didn't. You can't act like you broke up."

"Exactly," said Jessie. "Stew is the voice of reason. You can't be down, Duncan. You've made major tactical inroads with Carly."

"She knows your name," said Stew.

"She engages you in Kwik Mart–style pleasantries," added Jess.

"She knows you're a kind of a gump who can be easily pushed around," said Stew.

"That's huge, Duncan," said Jess. "*Huge.* She's not just going to forget you're a weenie."

"Thanks for the encouragement," Duncan said. He shut his locker and shook his head.

"Don't be so gloomy," urged Jess. "I can guarantee that no girl—not even beaver-loving activist Carly Garfield—likes her men chronically gloomy."

"I dunno," said Duncan. "I'm a wreck. Maybe I need to take antidepressants. My mom says they're just a crutch. What I really need is to find a friggin' bully."

"Can we back up just a sec?" said Stew. "Did I miss some crucial information about Carly and beavers?"

"They're rodents," said Jess. "Beavers. Just big rodents."

"Oh, I thought they were mammals," said Stew.

"Rodents *are* mammals, dumbass," she said, swatting him. "It's like that kingdom, phylum, class, order, family, da-da, da-da, da-dum stuff."

"I thought it was kingdom, class, phylum, fam—"

"No, asshat, it's king—"

"Okay, enough!" said Duncan. "The ACTs are in the past. And apparently Stew struggled with the science. But whatever. Let it go. We were talking about me and Carly."

"We do that a lot," snapped Stew.

First bell rang. Without another word passing between them, they shuffled off to different classrooms. Duncan kept his head down during Psychology class, making minimal eye contact with his teacher. He did attempt eye contact with Carly, but without success. She answered questions perkily, her attention focused either on taking notes or on Mr. Arnold's lecture. After class, she hurried away. Duncan tucked his books under his arm and walked lifelessly to the boys' lockers for gym.

Physical Education had definitely grown more tedious and humiliating over the years, he thought. To his eyes, Duncan appeared just as pasty and unmuscled as he'd been in fourth grade. All that had really changed about him was his height, and that had changed only marginally. He pulled the ill-smelling Owls T-shirt over his head, then changed into knee-length shorts. He was jostled slightly in the cramped locker room by Kurt Himes, a terminally suburban wannabe rapper removing necklaces and earrings.

"Hustle up, men!" barked Coach Chambliss, their gray-haired gym instructor. He insisted on being called "Coach" despite not coaching anything.

"That dude is old school," said Kurt under his breath.

"Coach is so old school, he poops eight-tracks," said Duncan.

Kurt laughed a snorty laugh.

"Tha's cold, bro."

Duncan walked out of the dank locker room and into the daylight, his head down, hair falling across his face. He and Kurt were among the last students to finish dressing. They crossed the running track and walked onto the practice field, where students had already arranged orange pylons into neat rows. Jessie was dragging a giant mesh bag of soccer balls.

"Hustle up, Mr. Boone!" shouted Coach Chambliss. "Hustle up, Himes! Double time, men!"

They broke into a light jog. Duncan caught up to Jessie and helped her lug the soccer balls to their rightful place in the center of the field.

"Thanks, Mr. Boone," she said.

"Just doing my part to make sure we all learn the fundamentals of soccer."

Coach Chambliss blew his whistle.

"Line it up!" he yelled. He spoke with the hyperalert cadence of a drill sergeant. Coach watched as his students formed two lines behind the pylons. "We have a new student joining us today, people, and I'd like to introduce him to every—"

He stopped midword and eyed Kurt.

As Kurt often did, and never with positive results, he held his hand over his crotch in a pseudo rapper pose.

"Is your penis bothering you, Mr. Himes?" asked Coach Chambliss.

Students giggled. Kurt quickly dropped his hands to his sides.

"N-nah, Coach," he stammered. "It's all good."

"Then do not touch it during class, Mr. Himes." Coach Chambliss glared at Kurt for several uneasy seconds, then blew his whistle again to silence the gigglers. "As I was saying before Mr. Himes touched himself, we are joined today by a new student. He's recently moved to Elm Forest from Bemidji, Minnesota. Excellent fishing in Bemidji—I myself have visited many times." Coach cleared his throat and looked for a new face in the group. "Wambaugh, Frederick!" he called. "Is there a Frederick Wambaugh here?"

A hand went up in the back row of students, no more than fifteen feet from Duncan and Jessie.

"Here," called a deep voice. "You can just call me Freddie."

"You are 'Mr. Wambaugh' in this class, Frederick," said Coach.

"It's *Wawhm*-baugh," said Freddie. "Not *Waim*-baugh."

More uneasy seconds followed.

"Mr. *Waim*-baugh, are you proficient at soccer?" asked Coach Chambliss.

"Nope," said Freddie, smirking.

"Well, you're here to learn. Please come up with Mr. Himes and demonstrate our first drill for your classmates, if you'd be so kind."

Freddie paused for a moment before lurching forward. He bumped unapologetically into a pair of students as he moved toward Coach. Jess elbowed Duncan and whispered, "Dude, the new kid is built like a *house*."

"He's at least a house," whispered Duncan. "Or a barn. Or a government building."

Freddie was massive. Maybe six foot five, Duncan reckoned, and two and a half spins on a scale. Freddie's giant feet were like frying pans, and his short black hair barbed like a cactus.

"Himes!" yelled the coach.

Kurt jerked forward and stood near Freddie, who absolutely dwarfed him. It reminded Duncan of a hippo and a small bird.

"This warm-up drill is so incredibly simple that even Mr. Himes and Mr. Wambaugh—a new student who has just confessed that he is *not* proficient at soccer—will be able to execute it flawlessly."

Coach walked briskly over to the mesh bag, withdrew a ball with his foot, and popped it into the air, catching it against his chest.

"You will find a partner, stand ten yards apart, and kick the ball back and forth crisply. I expect to see clean trapping and striking." He rolled the ball to Freddie. "Mr. Wambaugh will now propel the ball toward Mr. Himes, who will trap it with—"

Freddie—in a surprisingly quick and efficient motion—stepped forward, swung his right leg hard, and scorched the ball toward Kurt, hitting him in the groin. Every boy in class cringed and emitted an "ohwwow" sort of noise. The ball bounded away as Kurt crumpled.

"Mr. Wambaugh!" yelled Coach.

Freddie was bent over cackling.

"Mr. Wambaugh, I do not consider it amusing when students disregard safety in my class!" He pointed at Freddie as he walked over to Kurt. "Incidentally, I hope all of you noticed how Mr. Wambaugh's support foot was planted behind the ball on that kick. Thus, the ball was elevated and Mr. Himes couldn't . . ." He paused, watching Kurt whimper and roll on the ground. "Well, there wasn't much he could do."

Coach knelt down to speak softly to Kurt.

"Mr. Himes," he said, "at this time it *is* acceptable for you to place your hands over your crotch. But this is not a privilege I extend under normal circumstances. Do you understand?"

"Gughit," said Kurt quietly. He continued to squirm in the grass, moaning in pain.

Coach looked angrily at Freddie. "Mr. Wambaugh, please return to the locker room and await further instructions. I do not appreciate the attitude I've seen from you so far."

"Okeydokey, Coach Ch*aim*-bliss," said Freddie.

He continued chuckling as he walked lazily through the lines of students. On his way, he slugged Donovan Kelso in the arm—apparently for laughing too much—and subtly delivered a crippling wedgie to Tim Matsuzaka.

"Hustle, Mr. Wambaugh!" called Coach. "I expect you to jog!"

Freddie didn't.

"Oh. My. God," whispered Jessie.

"He's perfect," Duncan said.

She nodded. "He's beautiful."

"He has the gift."

"The best I've ever seen."

"The best," he agreed.

"*That* is your bully."

"That's the god of bullies."

"The golden god."

10

Duncan plopped down next to Stew at their usual lunch table.

"You're not dining with Friends of the Beaver today?"

"They're called TARTS," said Duncan. "And no, I am not. No direct invitation was extended. But Carly is still being cool."

Jessie slammed her fry-filled cafeteria tray down on the table directly across from Duncan. "Well, did you tell Stew all about him?" she asked, clearly thrilled. She dipped several fries into a pool of ketchup then stuffed them into her mouth.

"No, I haven't yet," Duncan said. "Stew was making beaver cracks again."

"Did you tell me about who?" he asked.

"Abugh da poofeh buwwy!" said Jess, chewing, fry bits falling out of her mouth.

"Um, one more time, please," said Stew.

Jess swallowed, then cleared her throat. "About the perfect bully," she said. "What are you, deaf?"

"He really was perfect," added Duncan. "In every possible way. Girth. Temper. Evident schadenfreude."

"He's German?" asked Stew.

"No, dumbass," said Jess. "Schadenfreude: to derive satisfaction from the misfortunes of others. That's our boy all right. So schadenfreudish. You should've seen this guy in gym, man. He'd only been playing soccer for *three friggin' minutes* before Chambliss kicked him off the field. But he left a trail of misery in his wake, and he walked away *laughing*. It was awesome." She crammed more fries into her mouth. "He hid Kurb righ innanads wif a baw!"

"Jess, stop talking with your mouth full," said an irritated Stew. "It's gross, and you make no sense."

She gulped down the fries, guzzled chocolate milk, and licked ketchup from her chin. The she belched.

"Gross," said Stew. "Pink-haired heifer."

Jessie snickered. "I *said* he hit Kurt right in the 'nads with a ball!" she repeated. "A total laser that put old Himes down for the rest of class."

"It was a solid kick," said Duncan, nodding.

"No way that dude will be able to reproduce," said Jess.

"Which is for the best," said Duncan.

"So what's this thug's name?" Stew asked. "And why have we never heard of him?"

"Freddie," said Jess. "Freddie Wambaugh. He's new to Elm Forest. But he is most definitely *not* new to bullying. This kid's had practice. Did we mention he's the size of a house?"

"It's true," said Duncan.

"You'll have to get the straight dope on Freddie from your mom," Jess said.

"Right," responded Duncan. "She has *S* through *Z*, so I assume Freddie is one of her students."

"Stew," said Jess, "this guy really was magical. The perfect thug for Duncan's purposes. He's more physically intimidating than ten Perry Hurleys."

"How's he compare to that Sloth dude?"

"Are you kidding me? Freddie eats a crunchy bowl of Sloths for breakfast every morning." She leaned across the table to emphasize her point. "There is absolutely no comparison. Freddie is the best there's ever been."

"And he's a new kid," said Duncan. "So he has no attachment to anyone in school—none whatsoever. This is key. He's the ideal candidate to terrorize me. Can you just imagine Carly's reaction if Freddie were to, like, cram me in a locker? That'd be awesome."

"Dude, she'd crawl in there and give you mouth-to-mouth," said Jessie. She and Duncan high-fived.

"How the hell are you going to get the universe's preeminent bully to work with you?" asked Stew. "Seems tricky."

"It does," agreed Duncan.

"Everybody wants somethin'" said Jessie matter-of-factly. "I'll bet Freddie is no different."

"Except for Sloth," said Duncan. "He wanted nothing."

"Nothing we could give him," countered Jessie. "That's all.

But a third-shift worker living alone in that cat-poop-box of an apartment probably wants *something*."

"Fair point," said Duncan. "So what do we think Freddie wants?"

"Hell if I know," she said. "You've gotta ask."

"You're the one who has a way with people," said Duncan. "You ask."

"But I am *not* the one trying to score with Carly Garfield." She wagged a finger. "And anyway, Freddie ain't people. He's scarier." She grabbed another handful of fries.

From a far corner of the cafeteria they heard a male voice scream, then breaking glass, and then the clatter of multiple trays against the floor. Soon after they heard cackling—the same cackling they'd heard during gym class.

"Ooh, that's our boy!"

Jessie stood and stared in the direction of the noises.

"Looks like he somehow took down half the boys' golf team," she said.

"It's okay," said Duncan. "They were expendable."

"Kenny Miessler got ketchup—wait, no, it's barbecue sauce—on his V-neck sweater."

"Is nothing sacred to Freddie?" said Duncan, smiling.

He and Stew were standing, too. They watched Freddie saunter toward a circular table in the corner of the cafeteria where the Goth kids and German exchange students sat. Freddie stood over them for a moment, his tray clutched in his right hand. He bent low, getting in the face of a black-haired nose-ring boy named Clint Chesbro.

"*Boo!*" yelled Freddie in a thunderous voice.

Clint fell back into his food. He and his friends abandoned the table. Freddie sat down, alone.

"That guy is freakin' *scary*," said Stew.

"Uh-huh," said Duncan. "We weren't kidding. We don't kid about important stuff like that."

"Think Clint's gonna go cast a level-four spell against Freddie?" asked Jessie.

"I don't think even the darkest Goth magic works against someone like that," said Stew. "Wow."

"Impressive," Duncan said. "I know."

"So go over there and ask him to help you, dude," said Stew. "Now's your chance. He's alone."

"Well, I can't just walk up to him in the cafeteria," said Duncan. "It's too public. He'd kill me with his spoon."

"Normally when you avoid confrontation, Duncan, I think you're wussing out," said Jessie. "But here you have a valid point. You've only got one shot with Freddie. If he turns you down cold, it's over. Period. Over. No more bully. And yeah, then he probably kills you with a blunt tool."

"So when are you gonna ask him for help?" asked Stew.

"You have to catch him alone," said Jessie. "This is imperative. Remember what a pushover Sloth was when no one was watching?"

"But Sloth really *is* a pushover," said Duncan. "Remember the lesson you learned? Judging books by their fur? Or something like that."

"Funny," she said. "But I bet that if we'd gone to talk to Sloth in the Maple North cafeteria, he would've behaved differently. There would've been no polite conversation over curry, no shy admission of his nonthreateningness."

"True," said Duncan. "I can see that. So we approach Freddie when he's alone."

"There you go with the *we* again," said Jessie. She'd finished her fries and had begun to lick ketchup from her fingers.

"C'mon," said Duncan, looking at her skeptically. "I'll do the talking—or at least I'll try—but you can't honestly expect me to approach him by myself. Seriously? That seems an unnecessary risk. Sure, he might be a bit more tame when he's alone. But the operative word there is *might*. He could also rip my torso from my legs, like Cage in Mortal Kombat."

"Freddie's a big dude," said Jessie, "but I don't think he has a Mortal Kombat–style signature fatality. He might be working on it, though. So fine, we'll go with you."

Carly briskly walked past Duncan's table. She looked at him, smiled, and waved with a quick twist of her wrist.

After she'd walked a few more feet, Stew slapped Duncan's back. "That was touching. Honestly, man. As someone who's known you for many years—someone who's seen more than a few pathetic displays from you regarding that chick—to see her acknowledge you directly"— Stew pretended to wipe a tear from his cheek—"maybe not with actual speech, but with eye contact . . . well, it's just really beautiful." He sniffed mockingly.

Jess reached a hand across the table as if to console Stew.

"Thank you," said Duncan, playing along. "I couldn't have come so far so fast without the support of my BFFs." He teased his green beans with a plastic fork. "In a few days I won't even get eye contact—not unless I can stir up a little more sympathy affection."

"Then we need to make the move on Freddie soon," said Jess.

"We don't know anything about him yet," said Duncan. "We've performed no research. No recon. We need to know his likes, his dislikes, his habits, his weakne—"

"He's on the move!" said an excited Stew.

Freddie was walking toward an exit. He'd left his tray at the lunch table. A cafeteria monitor began to approach him, then clearly thought better of it. Freddie threw open a set of double doors and left the lunchroom.

"We should follow him," said Duncan.

"We'll never catch up," said Jess. "And if we did, what would we do? The bell's about to go off, kids will flood the hallway, and then there's no talking to him. Because he really would rip you apart at the waist."

"Right. So how do we corner him?"

"Outside," she said. "Parking lot. After school. We'll locate his locker before the end of the day, then tail him."

"What if he takes the bus?" asked Duncan.

"Then today we take the bus." She thought for a moment. "No, actually *you* take the bus, Duncan. Stew and I will follow in my car. We maintain contact via cell. When Freddie gets off, you get off."

"What if the bus loses you?" asked Duncan.

"You think a school bus is going to try to *shake* me?"

"No, right, I guess not."

"Don't you have detention today, Jess?" asked Stew.

"Why, thank you, Stewart. Nice to know you're monitoring my disciplinary obligations. Yes, I do have detention penciled into the planner today. But I'm gonna go ahead and miss it, I think."

The bell rang. After lunch, Jessie quickly located Freddie's locker, then relayed its coordinates to Duncan and Stew. Classes came and went. Duncan exchanged pleasantries with Carly. She had the kindest smile, the most emotive eyes, the least insincere "How're you feeling, Duncan?" he'd ever heard. It wasn't quite the same as Friday's outflow of compassion, but it was good. Immediately following eighth period, Duncan, Stew, and Jess met at a predetermined location near—but not too near—Freddie's locker. Duncan felt like a small weaponless hunter stalking some enormous six-headed dragon.

They followed Freddie outside, maintaining a safe distance, so it was unlikely they would be noticed by their target. Much to Duncan's relief, Freddie walked past the row of buses and toward the student lot. He had a slow, ominous gait. Unhurried yet untiring, like the preternaturally evil killers in eighties slasher movies. The plodding pace actually made it difficult for them to follow Freddie sneakily. Stew and Jessie broke away from Duncan, circling around to the opposite side of the lot. They had decided not to approach Freddie as a group—"If he sees us come at him," said Jessie, "he's more likely to blow."

When he reached the asphalt of the student lot, Freddie slowed further. He scanned the parking area, seemed to identify his car, then walked toward it. Stew and Jessie crept along the tree line that bordered the lot. Duncan had moved himself to within twenty feet of Freddie, close enough to feel—or to imagine feeling—an aura of pure mean. They were heading toward an old, partially rusted black Monte Carlo that appeared to have a person waiting at the wheel. Duncan sped up.

"Hey, um . . . hello!" he called tentatively. "Freddie? Hello? I was wondering if I could have just a quick second."

Freddie turned slowly. His eyes were narrowed, his expression menacing. He balled his beefy hands into fists. Duncan stepped back to make sure he wasn't standing within arm's length. He'd lost sight of Stew and Jess.

"Oh, hi," Duncan said. "Welcome to Elm Forest, Freddie. You're new, right? I'm Duncan." He nervously cleared his throat. "Duncan Boone. I'm a junior here. We're in gym class together. Man, that Coach Chambliss sure is a bast—"

Turns out Duncan had underestimated the length of Freddie's arms.

In a swift, almost effortless motion, Freddie grabbed Duncan's shirt and flung him onto the trunk of the Monte Carlo.

Duncan made a faint *"ooooohh"* sound as he twisted through the air, then landed with a thud. Freddie pinned him against the car with his left forearm—which felt like an anvil—and kept his right hand available for pummeling.

"No time to chat, dweeb."

"Wow," said Jess, emerging from behind a yellow SUV. "That was just spectacular."

"Dude is good," said Stew, his head popping out from behind a shrub.

Freddie eyed them suspiciously. He grinned at Duncan, pressing him a bit harder against the hot metal of the Monte Carlo's trunk.

"Friends of yours, loser?"

"Y-yes," said Duncan. "We're a band. The Blow—whoops, no. We've changed our name. We're called Fat Barbie. We've been playing together for—"

"That's way more information than I need, dork."

Freddie shoved Duncan higher up onto the car and pressed his face against the rear windshield. Out of the corner of his eye, Duncan could see a small blond girl sitting in the front, watching the confrontation. She looked a little irritated.

Jess crept gingerly along the front end of the SUV.

"So," she said, "Duncan was just wondering if he could ask you something, Freddie. It's more of an offer, really—a good one."

Freddie loosened his grip slightly. "What a friendly school this is turning out to be," he said. He stared intently at Duncan's face. "Looks like you get yourself beat up from time to time. Maybe you shouldn't sneak up on people so much."

"You're absolutely correct," said Duncan. "There's no question. It was foolish. I regret my sneaking. Won't happen again." He paused. "The black eye is actually from a band-related garage accident, though. A speaker fell and—"

"Don't care, dingleberry. Not even a little."

The tiny blond girl's head poked out of the driver's-side window. "What the hell, Fred? Get in the car."

"Hold on," called Freddie. "This dorkball is trying to ask me something. I've gotta say no, and then I have to make him regret asking. So I'll be a minute."

"Oh, no," said Duncan. "No, don't say no until you've heard the pitch. Really. It's nothing too difficult. Minimal effort on your part. My friends and I, we have the greatest respect for your talent. You're the man."

"An artist," said Jessie.

"A natural," added Stew.

"We know," said Duncan. "We've been investigating the local bully population, and you're really off the map. What we saw today in gym? Let's just say we were impressed, Freddie—and you've impressed the right people."

Freddie, perplexed, loosened his grip a bit more, allowing Duncan to sit forward.

"I'll tell you what I'm looking for," he continued. "I need—for reasons that I can't really disclose—a bully. A personal bully. It's not like you'd be on my private staff or anything. I have no staff. I'm not made of money. But I'm looking to pay for à la carte bullying services."

Freddie stared.

"And I'm not looking for someone to bully *other* people on my behalf, just so you know," said Duncan. "Nothing like that. No, I need someone to bully *me*. Preferably around school, and at times that are mutually convenient. Starting, like, as soon as possible. All you really have to do is subject me to some prearranged abuse, and I'll give you, say, forty bucks?"

Freddie kept staring.

"Fifty?" asked Duncan. "Really, I have very limited resources, and most of it goes toward sound equip—"

"That's totally deranged, freak."

"But you'll consider it?"

"Look," said Freddie, "like you said, I'm a bully. We have a tradition of taking lunch money, property, valuables. Whatever we need, we take. There are income streams available to me. I don't need your cash."

"Fred!" yelled the blond girl, again sticking her head out the window. "I think it's great that you're trying to make new friends and all, but let's go."

"Just a seco—"

"Now!" she hollered. "Stop the violence, madman."

Freddie tossed Duncan from the trunk. "We're done," he said. "And if I bully you, it'll be for pleasure."

"So you won't help?"

"I'm not helpful," said Freddie, opening the car door.

"I can write a pretty mean comparative essa—"

Freddie slammed the door shut. The girl revved the Monte Carlo's engine, and Duncan stepped aside. Then he watched them back up and pull out of the lot.

"Bummer," said Stew.

"Total bummer," said Jessie. "The thugs aren't buyin' that comparative essay stuff you're sellin'."

"I think I'm lucky to be alive," said Duncan. "That crazy chick at the wheel saved my life." He watched the Monte Carlo speed away from school. "But yeah, bummer. Now I'm finished."

Duncan sulked on the ride home (though he tried to appear somewhat cool), sulked upstairs to his room (though he tried to seem stoic and emotionless), and sulked as he emptied the contents of his backpack onto his bed (alone, he was just himself: bummed). He fell into the chair at his desk, sulking, and played a somber mix of punk and power ballads on iTunes. Then he grabbed his journal from the mess of school trash.

I hope you got your fix of my analytical skills in Entry 11, 'cuz that's not on the menu today. . . .

EFTHS: where life can suck on a dime. As great as things were going—no, as f*#@!ng great as things were going—when I issued the previous update on my non-English-class life, that's how galactically bad things are going now. Without going into all the whys and hows and whos (although you can pretty much assume it involves a girl, given the blunt emotional extremes and the use of partially redacted profanity), let's just say that I am now feeling like Nick Carraway riding in the victoria with Jordan Baker. Except we're not in a stylish touring car, but a crappy Chrysler product with 140,000 miles on the odometer. And there's not actually a girl in the car at all, but more an idea of a girl.

"There are only the pursued, the pursuing, the busy and the tired."

I'm those last three.

Duncan's laptop made a fluttery beeping noise. An IM had arrived. He tossed the journal aside, then threw his pen at a bulletin board as if he were a circus knife-thrower. He sighed, then leaned over the keyboard to type.

CleanUpThatJess!:	sup dude. U were quiet on the ride home.
St4irw4y2Dunc4n:	Long day coulda ended w/ me dead in a parking lot. But I'm cool. Lotsa homework, tho. :O
CleanUpThatJess!:	I got the 5-0 on my ass. /swivels head nervously
St4irw4y2Dunc4n:	???
CleanUpThatJess!:	da po-po . . .
CleanUpThatJess!:	. . . the fuzz . . .
CleanUpThatJess!:	. . . the pigs. (police, yo). EFTHS called to tell the Pangers their daughter missed detention. so fine. but the Ps didn't exactly know about the most recent rules infraction. So oops . . .
St4irw4y2Dunc4n:	lol

He wasn't really laughing. Duncan sighed. He was still more or less sulking. He typed lazily.

St4irw4y2Dunc4n:	so u in trouble?
CleanUpThatJess!:	I'm no longer free to come and go. /rolls eyes, gags, flips dad off. Grrr.

St4irw4y2Dunc4n: rofl

Again, Duncan was not really rolling or laughing. He was just trying to seem not completely self-absorbed and frumpy. Although, in fact, he was both.

St4irw4y2Dunc4n: so can u still practice?

CleanUpThatJess!:   curfew @ 6 until I've served my time.

St4irw4y2Dunc4n: *@#! that gives Fat Barbie an hour a night, tops. that cuts deep into our BSing time.

Talia's small pigtailed head peeked into his room. "Hey, Mom says you've gotta come downstairs to eat, okay?"

"Sure thing, T," he said. "How was school today?"

"Fine," she said. "We're learning to play the recorder. There's going to be a concert and everything. Can I join your band if I get good?" She smiled.

"Totally," he said. "Our woodwind section is a little light."

Talia skipped away. Duncan spun back to the keyboard.

St4irw4y2Dunc4n: l8r, J. dinner calls . . .

CleanUpThatJess!:   eat your veggies, clean your plate, etc. /stuffs five nilla wafers into mouth.

Conversation over dinner was nonspecific, light, and surfacey. Except, that is, for a short exchange that involved Freddie.

"Hey, um . . . Mom," began Duncan. "What's the story with this new kid, Freddie Wambaugh? He's one of yours, right?"

His mom brought a forkful of asparagus to a halt halfway between her plate and mouth.

"What have you heard?" she asked. "Did he do something to you? Are you all right?"

"Yeah," said Duncan, looking at his food. "I'm totally fine. He did nothing. He's in my gym class, that's all. Freddie's first day of soccer with Coach Chambliss left three people wounded and the rest of us permanently scarred. He's a terrifying dude."

"Well, I'm not really allowed to discuss other students with you, Duncan. And you know that."

"Okay," he said. "Just curious, that's all."

"But yes," she added, "he is a sizeable person."

A brief silence followed.

"High school is scary," observed Talia.

"You have no idea," Duncan and his mom said simultaneously. She ate her asparagus while he swirled his mashed potatoes.

"So can you tell me where Freddie's from?" he asked his mother.

"Boundaries, honey." She chewed. "Weren't you just telling me about the importance of boundaries? Anyway, why not just ask him yours—?" She paused. "No, don't ask him. Avoid contact."

Another silence.

"Why is Coach Chambliss called 'Coach' anyway? Did he like the sitcom? Does he like expensive leather handbags?"

"He used to coach girls' softball."

"When?"

"About ten years ago, until . . ." She paused again, then rested her utensils on her plate.

"Until?" asked Duncan.

"Until an anger-management issue came to light." She cleared her throat. "Anyone need more ham?"

"Freddie seems to have those," said Duncan.

"Boundaries, honey," said his mom. "Boundaries."

12

The next day Duncan awoke to a grim reality: his face was almost entirely unblemished. A hint of a cut on the nose remained, as did maybe a slight bluish tint to the tiniest portion of his cheek. That was it, though. How many times had he actually *hoped* for this scenario, to wake up magically zitless and unmarked? Lots of times. But not that day. Without the bruises, the severe discoloration, the scabs that told a tale of fresh torture, what could he be to Carly? Nothing. Not a thing. Just another high school boy with petty, unidimensional needs.

"Ack," he said, inspecting himself in a small Limp Bizkit–themed mirror that he'd won at a carnival in, like, 1999. "Suddenly I'm a pretty boy."

He skipped breakfast. He text-messaged Jessie to say that he could drive himself to school. The ride was somber and lonely. He put in a home-produced CD of himself covering (or negligently attempting to cover) Zeppelin songs. He shook his head in despair and frustration as he parked his Reliant in the student lot. Duncan sat behind the wheel glumly. He looked in the rearview mirror, hoping that—just maybe—some stronger suggestion of a shadow of a memory of an injury had manifested itself. But no. He had mostly recovered.

"Crud."

He thought briefly about punching himself in the eye, but decided that he wouldn't have the nerve to follow through with any real force. Plus, it was possible that he wasn't capable of administering a black eye no matter how hard he tried—he hadn't punched anyone since slugging Jessie in kindergarten. And that incident ended with him flat on his back in the water table. So no hitting.

Carly's Prius pulled in next to Duncan's car. He averted his eyes from the rearview mirror. Not cool to let a girl see you checking yourself out, he thought. "Might as well get this over with," he mumbled to himself.

Duncan opened his car door as Carly opened hers.

"Mornin', Duncan," she said cheerily.

"Hey, Carly."

She was off like a bolt, taking long, quick strides through the parking lot. Duncan struggled to maintain her pace.

"Your face looks normal," she said, not slowing. "No more attacks, I guess?"

Duncan felt a wave of near-nausea. "Normal," she'd said. She couldn't at least say "better" or "nice" or "like a better-looking Brad Pitt" or anything else that was complimentary? No. "Normal" was all he got.

"No, no attacks," he said, too dejectedly. "Can't be too careful, though." He was already panting from the blistering speed at which Carly walked. "Jeez, you're sure"—Duncan took a deep, audible breath—"in a hurry."

"Yup," she said, not looking his way, and seeming to accelerate. "I'm leading these TARTS planning and organizational meetings every morning before school until the rally—we have the big rally in October that I've probably told you about. We're doing it in town to draw attention to the Elm Forest College fat-rat experiments. Which I've also probably told you about. So gross. The rally's at Watts Park, right by the . . ."

"—the statue of the dude on the horse?"

"Yeah, that's right. Did I tell you that, too?"

"Um . . . no. But, I mean, it's a logical spot. Great . . . vantage point for a speaker."

"Exactly. And for the band. We're getting a band. What a headache that is—don't get me started. But we're getting someone pretty big. We're talking to people in the hip-hop community, too. The district subcommittee on grassroots mobilization has been really helpful."

"Yeah, I hear, um . . . good things about those." Pant, pant, pant. "I'm in a band, you know."

"Hmm," she said. "Right, very cool."

"The Flaming Tarts," he said, feeling not quite in charge of his own mouth. "That's us. It's a tribute [panting] . . . to TARTS. Your TARTS, that is. I was telling [panting] . . . Jess and Stew about the rodents."

"That's so sweet of you!" she said, flinging open the school door. "'Kay, see you later. My meeting's in Wiggins's class-room."

"I'd really be interested in going, actually, if you . . ."

"Later," she said, waving, already ten feet away.

Duncan breathed deeply. He stood in his school's hotel-ish entry space and paused to take inventory of whatever he'd done or said, and to assess any damage: (1) He'd disclosed an uncanny awareness of the features and layout of Watts Park. Not terrible, unless Carly remembered the spaz-waving inci-dent. (2) He'd displayed a startling lack of cardiovascular fitness. So she knew she could beat him in a footrace. Not a big deal. Unless she was actually worried that he might some-day chase her. Hmm. (3) He'd changed the band's name to something stupid and vaguely culinary. "Oh, God," he mut-tered. Then he quickly decided that until the band had a gig, any name was just superfluous. So fine.

He bowed his head and began to plod slowly toward his locker. Despite Carly's indifference to him—and despite the fact that she and all her belongings were covered with anti-rodent-testing slogans—Duncan was more infatuated than ever. His recent, relatively brief glimpse into Carly's world had been completely thrilling. But he could feel her interest wane. He sighed, feeling doomed.

Then he felt a firm hand grip his collar.

From somewhere over his right shoulder, he heard the door to a restroom being thrown open. Then he briefly experienced the odd sensation of backwards flight, not unlike what he'd felt the day before when he'd been tossed onto a car trunk by . . .

"I've been rethinking your offer, dork," said Freddie. "And I think there *is* something you can do for me."

Duncan found himself pressed up against the algae-green tile of the boys' restroom. Freddie's left arm was pinned firmly to Duncan's neck, and his right hand still held the collar of his T-shirt. Duncan was still adjusting to the powerful smells of urinals, mildew, and heavily perfumed soap when Freddie got in his face.

"You're paying attention, right?"

"Sure, um . . . yes, Freddie. Strict attention." Duncan's eyes focused on Freddie's snarled, twitchy mouth.

"Okay. Try to stay with me here, dweeb. You're in a band, yeah?"

"Oh, yes," said Duncan. "Yes I am. Fat Bar—" He laughed slightly. "The Flaming Tarts. We've had a recent name change. But it didn't affect our core principles. We're still kind of a mixture of hard-edged, psychedel—"

"Yeah, 'cuz I care. Look, I need you to let my sister Syd in your band. She's your new guitarist."

"Actually, Freddie, I'm the lead guitari—"

"*Syd* is your new guitarist," Freddie said slowly, pushing harder against Duncan's neck. "Maybe you're not familiar with the bully-victim dynamic, dinkus. See, I tell you what you're going to do, then you do it. There's no asking, no thinking about it. You just do it. This is one of those can't-refuse things."

"Wait," said Duncan. "Are you threatening to beat me up if I don't agree to let you beat me up? Honestly, I don't see how I can lose this one."

Freddie was clearly irritated. And maybe a bit confused. "Just put my sister in your band, turd!" he finally said. "Or I'll not beat you up. At all. Ever. It'll be the worst nonbeating of your life. And it'll suck. In fact, I'll *protect* you. Then no one will beat you up."

"Well, has she ever play—?"

Duncan suddenly was airborne again. He struck a support column between two bathroom stalls, rattling the doors, then sank to the cold floor. He shook his head.

"All righty," he said. "So she's in the band. Great news. Really happy to have her. We'll probably practice tonight after school—my house at four forty-five, if that's convenient. I'll draw you a map to give to her. If that time doesn't—"

"Okay, dorkwad. Thanks."

Freddie began to clomp away.

"Hey, so, um, Freddie?" said Duncan, beginning to stand. "When do you think you might be able to assault me some-place else? Like, someplace with an audience? Can we start today?"

"Oh, sure thing. How 'bout I beat your ass in gym? That Chambliss guy'll go nuts again!" Freddie grinned and rubbed his hands together. "It'll be excellent."

"Actually, that's not the right crowd," said Duncan. "Can we do lunch?"

"Okay, suit yourself." Freddie walked to the restroom exit, then turned again. "Face or gut?"

"What?" asked Duncan.

"When I hit you, chump. Face or gut?"

"Oh, great question!" exclaimed Duncan. "Thanks for asking. Very considerate. Neither."

"Hey, dork, that's how I operate," said Freddie. "I slug people. I don't tease, I don't taunt. I hit. I shove. I occasionally kick people, but it's rare."

"You throw people," Duncan added.

"That I do," said Freddie proudly. "That I do. It's a sweet feeling when I get a dude vertical. Like you on the hood yesterday—that was nice. You're a flyer, dude. What are you, anyway? About a hundred fifty pounds? One fifty-five?"

"Yeah, somewhere in there, I guess," said Duncan.

"That's perfect. You get nice air and you still make a big noise when you hit stuff."

A pair of letterman-jacket-wearing boys walked into the restroom laughing.

"Out!" bellowed Freddie.

They jumped, spun, and scrambled away.

"So," said Duncan, "I suppose you could throw me around the cafeteria. That might work. I seem to rebound well."

"Cool," said Freddie. "You wanna give me a sign or something when it's go-time?"

"Oh, right. I'll throw a peace sign." Duncan raised his fingers to form a *V*. "That'll mean it's on."

Freddie nodded, flashed a peace sign back, then whistled as he left the restroom.

Duncan exhaled, then smiled to himself, then felt the rush of imminent, life-altering success.

Morning classes dragged on interminably. He watched clocks. He fidgeted, buzzing with excitement. "Chill out, spaz," said Jessie during a soccer scrimmage. Duncan couldn't. He'd been assigned to play fullback, a strictly defensive position that required him to linger back near his goal. But instead, he sprinted up and down the field like a rabid pony. "Mr. Boone, you are out of *position*!" screamed Coach Chambliss.

Duncan's team lost 9–0 in a fifteen-minute game. He left the field drenched in perspiration, but not yet tired. He was desperate for the bullying to begin, and—if luck and Carly's altruism were on his side—to worm his way back into some inner sphere of her social/academic/activist life.

God, he liked the thought of that.

"Nice game today, Beckham," said Jessie as she caught up with Duncan between periods.

"Thanks," he said.

"I was being ironic. Because you suck."

"Oh, right. Well, the important thing is giving your best effort, right?"

"I think not sucking is the important thing."

"Well, you can't have both," he said, grinning.

"Why the good mood?" asked Jessie. "You rockin' the Zoloft?"

"Nope," he said. "Freddie and I have reached an accord."

"No *way*!" said Jessie. "So when do you brawl?"

"Lunchtime."

"What was his price? Fifty? More?"

"Actually," began Duncan, "it wasn't a monetary arrange—" The bell rang, cutting him off. "Tell you about it later."

He walked away with unnecessary haste. Jessie stood in the hallway with a perplexed expression. In his giddy anticipation of fake-bullying, Duncan had failed to think through the ramifications of adding a fourth band member without consulting Stew and Jess. They might—no, they *would*—be righteously mad, he realized. After all, the group was not solely Duncan's thing. They'd collectively decided to form the band—it was, in most ways, an organic result of a longtime friendship. Adding another person was no small move, and it certainly wasn't something that Duncan had any particular right to do. Oh yeah, and he'd also changed the band's name again. Hmm.

"Can't stress," he told himself, attempting a pep talk. "First get yourself harassed, then get the girl, then notify the band of various changes."

Duncan sat through another forty-nine-minute class that only seemed to last a month. Then: lunchtime. Assuming Freddie upheld his part of the bargain (which didn't seem certain, given that Freddie was a goon), Duncan would soon be completely humiliated in front of a huge percentage of the school's student population. Hopefully, this public emasculation would go over well with Carly. Duncan was all in. He would walk away from this particular lunch either totally ruined or totally victorious. Or maybe, if Freddie was too enthusiastic, he wouldn't walk away at all. But Duncan had decided this was a risk worth taking.

A hairnetted cafeteria worker slammed a serving spoon down on his plate, dislodging a thick mass of au gratin potatoes. Duncan then accepted a fishwich, peas, a Jell-O cup, and a half-pint of milk. He stepped into the main lunchroom and paused, standing beside a Coke machine, and scanned the area for the relevant parties.

Freddie, being the largest, was easy to spot. He was standing next to the circular table that used to belong to the Goth-and-German contingent, arms folded across his thick chest. He returned Duncan's glance with an almost imperceptible nod. Duncan continued to survey the room, looking for Carly. His eyes swept over an excessively giddy Stew and Jess. They sat in the usual spot, waving excitedly. Duncan searched for some sign of Carly amid the cafeteria clamor. Looking, looking . . .

There she was, walking just a half step ahead of a cluster of handmaids. And she was radiant. On most occasions, Duncan would have been content to simply stand and watch her walk, sit, eat, and converse in that perfectly graceful way of hers. But not that Tuesday. He made eye contact with Freddie, then stepped forward, moving with haste along a line that would intersect with Carly's path at the center of the cafeteria. Freddie was moving, too.

"Wait for it," Duncan said softly to himself. "Wait for it. Wait, wait . . ."

He drew close to Carly. It all felt so fantastically clandes-tine, so fictional, so Matt-Damon-hanging-from-a-helicopter. Just a few more steps and . . .

"Hi, Duncan!" called his mother.

Her voice hit him like a blow-dart from the brush.

"Mom? Errr . . . hey."

He spun around to see her walking alongside another guidance counselor, Evelyn Whitman, and carrying a pile of papers and folders in her arms. She didn't stop to chat—which was nice, what with Freddie approaching and ready to maul him. Duncan shook his head and glanced at Freddie, who stopped in his tracks, evidently confused. Or perturbed. Carly took a seat at a table with her TART friends.

This is no problem, Duncan thought. Just wait for Mom to leave. She *can't* witness the beating. Wait . . . wait . . .

He watched her.

And watched.

C'mon. Step lively, Mom.

But she stopped to have a word with Jeremy Voskil, a whip-smart future valedictorian.

Ack! Come *on*, Mom. Wait . . . wait . . .

Duncan stood looking dazed and lost. A few students looked up at him quizzically. He drifted closer to Carly's table. She still hadn't noticed him. Freddie followed. Duncan drifted a little more, waiting.

Soon she was back on the move, nearing the doors that led to the guidance area. When she opened them and left the lunchroom, Duncan's right arm shot out low at his side and he flashed the peace sign. Then he braced himself in preparation for a feeling that had grown a little too familiar: air travel on school property.

Freddie's large paw again seized Duncan's collar. Another hand grabbed his belt. Hmm, new method, thought Duncan. Freddie spun him around once—sending bits of potato flying in all directions—then lofted him onto a sparsely populated table. Beverages spilled, trays and plates crashed against the floor, students scattered. Duncan slid down the length of the table on his back, managing to catch hold of the edge with his left hand to prevent sliding off.

"Hey!" he managed in mock indignation, scrambling to his feet. He could distinctly hear clapping and laughing from the section of the cafeteria occupied by sporty morons. He heard shocked gasps from almost everyone else. No security, faculty, or cafeteria monitors in sight.

Freddie approached Duncan with a smirk on his wide face. He towered over him. "Whoops," Freddie said.

He gave Duncan's shoulder a shove.

"Watch where you're going, dweeb." He shoved Duncan again, then took a dollop of orange Jell-O and smeared it across Duncan's forehead. Freddie smiled. "You should apologize," he said. Another shove followed.

Oh, Freddie's good, thought Duncan. Very good. Or else he's completely forgotten it was a setup.

"Fight, fight!" chanted a small but inspired group of jocks.

This seemed to stir the lunch police to action. School staff began to home in on the confrontation.

So did Carly.

A poppy-seed bagel struck Freddie in the head, startling him. He turned around just in time to take a carrot stick to the face.

"Hey!" Freddie said, shielding his eyes with his hands.

Carly brushed past him and grabbed Duncan by the hand. Then she zipped another carrot at Freddie's back.

"Aaaah!" he said, spinning around.

Carly spoke to Freddie slowly, as if to a dog. "Leave . . . him . . . alone." She stared.

Freddie sneered.

"No one's impressed," she said.

"Not even a little?" said Freddie smart-assedly.

"Walk away, dude," called the plaintive voice of Perry Hurley. "She's not playing."

"If you really need to pick on someone," Carly said, still glaring at Freddie, "I'm right here."

Duncan looked down at his T-shirt—a personal favorite, the Zeppelin at the Fillmore West concert shirt. It was covered in various sticky liquids. He looked at Carly, her adorable face flashing anger at Freddie. The shirt is an acceptable casualty, he thought.

"Cripes' sake, what's going on here?" said a shaky Harry Drago, an ancient shop teacher.

Carly gestured at Freddie. "This idio—"

"An accident!" blurted Duncan. "My bad. All my fault. I'm just totally clumsy. It's all on me." Duncan felt that the least he could do in the wake of Freddie's masterful debut as his personal bully was to protect him from official discipline.

Carly gave Duncan a puzzled glance, then spoke up again. "But this big creep just toss—"

"All my fault!" repeated Duncan. "Really. All me."

The teacher looked around at the carnage: broken plates, milk slicks, utensils, mounds of food.

"I'm really very sorry," said Duncan.

"You oughta be," said Mr. Drago. He began to shuffle away, beckoning a member of the janitorial staff to the scene.

Carly held Duncan's hand. "Why would you cover for that guy, Duncan?" she asked. "Is that the bully who mashed your face up?"

"Yeah, well . . . I think so," he said.

"And you're afraid that if you get him in trouble, he'll only treat you worse?"

"Well, something like tha—"

Carly pulled him close and squeezed. "Oh, that's awful," she said.

Duncan sprouted an involuntary grin. With his head resting momentarily on Carly's shoulder, he saw Jess and Stew in the distance laughing, high-fiving, and making obnoxious kissy faces.

"Here," said Carly, "sit with us, Duncan."

She led him by the hand to the TARTS table. They stepped

around the debris that remained from the confrontation with Freddie—a confrontation that had been executed flawlessly.

"You guys remember Duncan, right?" Carly asked her friends. They nodded, smiled politely, and greeted him. He sat down next to Carly. She gathered up napkins and began to peel chunks of food off him.

13

Having Carly Garfield remove flecks of food from his hair, as if she were a gorilla grooming her mate, was unequivocally the greatest moment in Duncan's life. He couldn't imagine what might've been the second greatest moment, either. Because watching Carly scrape tiny bits of fishwich from him with her nails was, like, orders of magnitude better than anything he'd ever experienced.

Did the fact that he'd elaborately deceived her lessen the thrill? Hell no.

At least not in any detectable way. All love rested on a shifting bedrock of deception, he told himself. His dad had said something like that once—maybe after dropping $3,200 on a TV without consulting Duncan's mom.

But whatever. The important thing was this: Carly was dotingly picking hardened cafeteria gruel from Duncan's hair. It was magical. As she did this, she talked almost dreamily about the upcoming TARTS rally. The substance of the conversation was really lost on Duncan, though. He merely enjoyed watching Carly's eyes move over his face. He responded to nearly everything she said with either "uh-huh" or an inquisitive "really?"

When all the obvious food particles had been extracted from Duncan's head and clothes, Carly began to involve Duncan in conversation with her friends, the small pod of girls—who turned out to be named Marissa, Chloe, Zoe, Sophie, Kylie, and Hayley—that he had thought of as handmaids. They all seemed fairly standard-issue to Duncan, gossipy, flaky, and vapid. They clearly weren't so zealous about TARTS—or any other socially responsible cause—as Carly was. In fact, the whole TARTS clique was something of a Carly Garfield cult of personality, a thing that existed because people wanted to get close to her.

Duncan, for example, wanted to get close to her. Thus began his assimilation into the Elm Forest Township High School chapter of Teens Against Rodent Test Studies.

"You'd better see about getting a less gooey shirt or something," Carly said to him, smiling. "Before the bell rings."

"Oh, right," he said, grinning back at her. "Less gooey is good. I'll shoot for that." He stood. "Hey, thanks again for intervening with that big dude. Dunno why he's got it in for me."

"Bullies are all the same, Duncan," she said. "They just care about preserving the feeling of power. The way they do it is to make everyone else feel weak." She rubbed his arm. "But you're not weak, Duncan."

Okay, that was kinda freaky/flaky, he thought.

But still cool in an oh-my-God-this-cute-flaky-girl-is-*rubbing-my-arm*! way.

"Thanks," he said, then walked away. Then he glanced back. Then walked. Then glanced again. He was deeply smitten. He strode toward Stew and Jess, then sat down.

"Wow," he said, his eyes wide.

"Dude!" chirped Jessie. "That actually worked. The incredibly convoluted, bordering-on-nonsensical plan worked."

"Tip of the cap to Freddie," said Stew. "Dude has some impressive dramatic skills."

"Yup, no doubt," said Jessie. "He clearly has many gifts: acting, bullying . . . um . . . Okay, he has exactly two gifts. But he really excels at those two things."

"Wow," Duncan repeated. He shook his head.

"Carly was touching your face there, buddy," said Stew.

"I know," said Duncan. "Wow. I know."

"I thought Freddie was gonna beat you down in front of your mom, dude," said Jess. "And then I thought she'd go all Miyagi and start karate-choppin' Freddie. Because that woman will defend her baby."

"Wow," said Duncan, still dazed by the thoroughness of his success. "I need to change my shirt. Carly said to."

"And if she told you to try to drink a gallon of milk in an hour, would you do it?" asked Stew.

"Yes, no question," he said. "Yes, I would. Even though I've already tried it, and it made me throw up, like, seventeen times, yes. Yes, I would drink a gallon of *anything* for Carly Garfield."

"Syrup?" asked Jess.

"Sure."

"Paco's secret *Muy Caliente* sauce?"

"I'd try, yes."

"Mayonnaise?"

"That's pretty viscous. Not sure it qualifies as a drink."

"It comes in gallon jars, though."

"But I'd have to eat it with a spoon. And when you have a spoon in your hand, you're not really drinking."

"Fine," said Jessie. "How 'bout spit?"

"My own, sure."

"How 'bout spit of unknown ori—?"

"Enough!" exclaimed Stew.

"Okay," said Duncan. "It might be an overstatement to say I'd drink anything. The point is, I would do some crazy stuff for Carly Garfield." He sighed contentedly.

"Like ruin your favorite shirt and embarrass yourself before a few hundred of your peers," said Jessie. "Just for example."

"Right. Like that. Speaking of which, I need to go change."

"Because Carly said."

"That's exactly right, Stew. I think I've got an extra gym shirt in my locker. If not, I still have those borrowed band costumes in the car—meant to return 'em."

"So you might have to wear a musty tuxedo shirt?" asked Jess.

"It was supposed to be an *Edwardian* shirt, not *tuxedo*. Like Jimmy Page wore. But yeah, I might go that route."

"Better to have a cool shirt with caked-on food than a shirt that's unsoiled but Edwardian," said Jess. "Not to mention stolen."

Duncan laughed happily.

"Fat Barbie is practicing tonight, yeah?" asked Stew.

"Yup," said Duncan.

There was still the pesky name-change issue to address, he thought. Oh, well. Later.

"Remember," said Jess, "I'm on double-secret parental probation. Detention after school, then home by six. I now live under strict rules. It sucks. So let's everyone be ready to play."

"Right," said Duncan. "Absolutely. Ready."

Oh, yeah. There was also the issue of Freddie's sister what's-her-name joining the band. That needed to be discussed. But later, he thought. This moment is too good to spoil.

Duncan got up from the table and began to walk toward an exit, careful to avoid Freddie's side of the cafeteria. After seeing the condition of his clothes, a sympathetic lunchroom monitor allowed him to leave. He walked through the empty halls grinning. He grew wistful passing classrooms that he'd sat in as a freshman and sophomore, places where he'd either gazed at Carly or daydreamed about her. All the long years of seemingly hopeless obsession had led, ultimately, to something spectacular. And Jess and Stew always thought I was being pathetic and silly, he thought. Hah. Goal-oriented and determined is more like it.

Upon reaching his locker, Duncan dug through a mound of scholastic miscellany until he found the spare gym shirt—

relatively clean, if heavily wrinkled. He removed the Zeppelin shirt slowly; it clung to his skin in places where cafeteria goo had hardened. Then he slipped the gym shirt on and stretched it a bit, hoping to make it slightly more roomy. He had little success. He looked at a hallway clock. Approximately four minutes until the bell would ring. He ripped a page from a spiral binder and snatched a pen from his backpack. Duncan rested the paper against his locker and began to scribble:

> F— Excellent show today. Well done. Really perfect.
> Couldn't have gone better. Thumbs-up. Hope your
> sister can meet us at 4:30. Address is 402 Wheatland
> St., two blocks north of the Citgo. Meet in the garage.
> Thanks! D

Was that too girly? he wondered. Eh. No time to edit. Duncan folded the note into a neat triangle, then rushed to Freddie's locker. The bell rang just as he was stuffing the note through a ventilation slot. Duncan hurried off—he certainly couldn't be seen conspiring with the thug who'd just harassed him. Plus Duncan wanted to get back to his own locker to chat with Carly.

A tangled web, he thought. But it's catching me the perfect bug.

Carly seemed tickled to see him after lunch. She touched his gym shirt, running her hand lightly down the shoulder.

"Better," she said, smiling.

Duncan was thrilled. Amazed. Agog.

Each short break between classes that afternoon was more delightful than the last. Carly, having actually witnessed Duncan being victimized, was treating him as if he were an adorable mouse she'd rescued from a laboratory—and not a fat one. That is to say, she was fawning over him: petting, smiling, giggling. She asked if he wouldn't like to attend a brief TARTS recruitment presentation after school in the auditorium. She'd been posting brightly colored notices about it all day, but was afraid no one would show.

"Oh, yeah," he said enthusiastically. "I'd be delighted."

"Great!" she said cheerily.

Duncan sighed another happy sigh. The TARTS thing would be short, Carly had said. Twenty minutes, tops. Plenty of time for him to get to get to Fat Bar—um, the Flaming Tarts' practice. Besides, Jessie had detention to serve.

As it turned out, the TARTS thing certainly *could* have lasted twenty minutes or less. After an appalling slideshow, featuring obese rodents dragging themselves slowly through a maze, and few short statements by Carly and Dr. Wiggins, they were ready to distribute pamphlets and adjourn. But then they asked if anyone had questions. Duncan, wishing to appear completely engaged, raised his hand.

"So which local labs and institutions, other than Elm Forest College, of course, have the worst track record with respect to rodent experimentation?"

Carly beamed, then quickly became serious, answering the question by rattling off a list of Midwestern universities and corporations.

Duncan raised his hand again. "What are the cage conditions like for most lab rodents?"

Again, Carly answered thoughtfully and thoroughly.

By the end of her answer, Duncan's hand had shot up again. And then again. And again. And again. He peppered Carly with questions, and she seemed to appreciate it. Eventually, Dr. Wiggins as well as all the other TARTS members and recruits left the auditorium. But Duncan and Carly remained, he in a plush front-row seat and she at a podium. Their Q and A lasted an hour; then they walked together to their cars, which, of course, were parked side by side. Duncan pretended to be fearful of another Freddie attack.

"You're not alone," said Carly. She put a hand on his shoulder.

Duncan blushed. "Thanks."

They conversed awhile longer in the parking lot; then Carly hugged him good-bye. *Hugged him!* Like with both arms squeezing. It was breathtaking.

Literally, he had breathing issues, he was so happy. He began to hyperventilate as he opened the Reliant's door. Carly had already smiled, given him a wiggly-fingered wave, and driven off, so she didn't actually see a light-headed Duncan sitting at the wheel of his car, his head between his knees taking deep, calming breaths.

That was just spectacular, he thought.

He inserted his key in the ignition and started the Reliant. The digital clock blinked 5:02.

"Whoops," he said aloud.

He sped out of the EFTHS parking lot, rather recklessly eased through a few stop signs, and raced home. When he arrived at his driveway, he saw Jessie's car parked along the street.

"Oh, man, she's gonna be *mad*," he said.

Then, just ahead of her car, he saw a black Monte Carlo— the same car Freddie had left school in the day before, the very Monte Carlo that he'd been tossed onto.

"Freddie's sister," said Duncan. "Oh, yeah." He stared at the garage. "Wonder how practice is going." He approached the side door of his garage with dread. He took note of the flaking brown paint, knowing that his dad would make him paint in the spring. He stood at the closed door and listened. He thought he heard laughter. Anxiously, he turned the door-knob and entered.

"Hey, everybody, really sorry I'm late. Couldn't be helped. There was this TARTS thing that Carly invited me to, and I couldn't very well say—"

A cowbell whizzed past his ear.

14

"Hey!" yelled Duncan. "Not this again!"

"*Yes*, this again!" shouted Jessie, flinging a strand of sleigh bells at him. "What the heck, dude?! It's like a quarter after five! You *know* I've gotta be home by six!"

"I'm sorry!" he said. He ducked to avoid a flying Cabasa. "I'm really, truly, incredibly sorry!" He remained hunched over near the door, unwilling to lift his head until he could be sure he wouldn't be struck by anything. "Enough with the projectiles!" he called. "Please! You're gonna break all the instruments! Or you'll break me!"

"Okay," said Jessie. "Fine, cease fire."

He stood up slowly. A set of castanets hit him in the stomach.

"Hey!" he yelled.

"Well, I hadn't actually hit you yet," Jess said. "And anyways, have I *ever* fought fair? No."

In addition to Jessie and Stew, Duncan saw a strangely familiar face in his garage. It belonged to the blond girl who'd been at the wheel of the Monte Carlo. Duncan immediately noticed that she had a red Scorpio-Blaster Flying V guitar slung over her shoulder. Impressive, he thought. She had surprisingly soft features for a Wambaugh. She also looked the part of a punk rock goddess: Replacements concert shirt, ripped jeans, Doc Martens, tousled hair. She had a burning heart tattooed on her left biceps, too, which impressed Duncan more than a little.

"Hi," he said to the girl. "You must be . . . ?"

"Freddie didn't even tell you my name?" she asked incredulously. "What a friggin' dope my brother is."

"No, he must've told me and I just forgot it. Really sorry."

"So you're the dope," she said.

"Right. Something like that. I'm Duncan."

"I'm Sydney," she said, smiling faintly. "People just call me Syd."

"So there's a new person in the band, Duncan," said Stew with mock calm. "Did you know this? I suppose an e-mail went out and I just missed it. Or maybe a memo was circulated. Or maybe it was in the band's newsletter and somehow I overlooked it. Oh, well."

"Sorry," said Duncan, pressing his hands together. "I really am. I totally meant to tell you guys. You were not supposed to find out by—"

"—meeting Syd for the first time while she was breaking into your garage?" asked Stew. "No, I doubt we were supposed to find out that way."

"Again, I'm really sor—" He paused. "Syd broke into the garage?" He looked at the new guitarist. "You broke into the garage, Syd?"

"Well, I *would* have broken in if these guys hadn't shown up and opened the door. Good thing they did, too. I guess there's an alarm. Hee-hee."

"Yeah, good thing. Why wouldn't you just go to the front door of the house?"

"There was a note. Freddie gave it to me. 'Meet in the garage,' it said."

"Exactly. It did not say 'Meet in the garage, but if it's locked, break in.' Who *does* that?"

"Um . . . people who want to avoid yet another conversation with their guidance counselor?" offered Syd.

"Ah, right," said Duncan. "I can see that being awkward." He looked at Stew and Jess. "So let me get this straight: you two guys see a strange person breaking into my garage—the place where we keep, like, hundreds of dollars' worth of instruments and sound equipment—and you let them in?"

"What were we supposed to do?" asked Jess. "Tackle her?"

"Well, maybe. Tackling seems appropriate."

"She didn't give off a burglar vibe, Duncan," said Stew. "She had a guitar with her. If she were going to break in and take sound equipment, would she bring her own guitar?" Stew paused, glancing away. "And she turns out to be pretty cool."

Duncan looked at the three of them.

"So," he said hesitantly, "she's cool enough that you two guys aren't mad at me for adding someone to the band without asking? She's *that* cool?"

"Hey," answered Stew, "as long as she can play."

"And, um . . . can she?" asked Duncan.

"We haven't really jammed," said Jessie. "We've been introducing ourselves to the new guitarist. Since you weren't here to make a formal introduction."

"Sorry," he said. "Once again. Very sorry."

"Not an issue," said Jess. "We like her. I think we've pieced together the important details of this whole covert deal between you and Freddie."

"It was Freddie's idea," said Duncan.

"Yeah," said Syd, "big idea man, my brother."

"In any case," said Jessie, "it turns out this chick has excellent taste. She's a connoisseur of the eighties Minneapolis rock scene, which I appreciate deeply." Jess pointed to the Replacements T-shirt. Syd struck a coquettish modeling pose. "A girl after my own heart," said Jess, grinning.

"Nice," said Duncan, plugging his guitar into an amp.

"So," he said, "maybe we can play, um . . . well, anything, I guess. Just to establish a musical rapport. What do you know, Syd?"

She shrugged. "Hmm. I've been trying to teach myself a few Stones songs. I haven't mastered anything, but I'm getting the hang of a few of 'em."

"Cool, great. Give us a taste of something."

"Okay," she said. "I've been working on 'Rocks Off.' Know it?"

"*Exile on Main Street,*" said Stew. "Very nice. Best album ever, if you want my opin—"

"Oh, come *on!*" said Duncan. "It's a great record, but seriously. Best *ever*? It's no *Houses of the Holy*. It's no *Zeppelin IV*. Hell, it's no *Zeppelin I*, eith—"

"Enough!" said Jessie. "Let's just let the girl play. I've gotta leave for home in, like, five minutes. Can we all just agree that 'Rocks Off' is a kick-ass song, and we'd love to hear Syd's version?"

"It's a totally kick-ass song," said Stew. "In fact, I'd say it's the best opening song on any album, ever. Hands down, the bes—"

"*Puh-leez!*" said Duncan. "Better than 'Black Dog'? I don't think so. Better than 'Good Times Bad Times'? You've gotta be kid—"

"Dudes!" yelled Jessie, smashing a drumstick against a cymbal. "Let the girl play."

"Oh, right," said Duncan.

"Sorry," said Stew.

"So," began Syd, "are practices always this, um . . ."

"Full of disagreement, violence, and very little music?" asked Jess. "Yes, pretty much. I'd say you're witnessing a pretty typical practice. Normally I yell a bit more." She smiled. "Hope that's not a problem."

"No, I admire loud women," said Syd. She and Jess fist-bumped. Syd then swung her guitar forward. She looked slightly awkward arranging her delicate fingers, Duncan noted. She cleared her throat nervously, then spread her feet wide.

"Okay," she said tentatively. "'Rocks Off,' here goes . . ."

To say that she sounded awful is an insult to guitarists who are merely awful. Syd sounded like an implement of torture. No, she sounded like the suffering victim of an implement of torture. She was excruciatingly slow and screechy. Whatever she was playing, it wasn't the scorching opener from *Exile*. It was more like something that should be played on an endless loop in Hell. And, to make matters slightly worse, she kept making guitar faces, scrunching up her eyes. She shook her head. Her mouth opened and closed operatically. Duncan felt a little queasy.

When the drums were supposed to enter, Jess did nothing but stare. When a vocalist was supposed to jump in, Duncan blurted, "Okay, okay!" into a floor-stand microphone, then walked toward Syd.

She stopped playing and smiled sheepishly. "What's up?" she asked, her warm green eyes looking up at Duncan. "Man, I just love that song."

"Yeah," said Duncan. "Me, too." And I hate to see it treated this way, he thought. "Solid, um . . . solid effort there, Syd. Very passionate. Really, um . . . committed."

"Thanks!" she said.

Jessie and Stew were simply looking at Duncan. Jessie seemed halfway amused. Stew seemed peeved.

"Hey, Syd," said Jess. "Come inside with me. I totally need a Mr PiBB before I leave. I'll introduce you to Mrs. Boone."

"Dude, I've met Mrs. Boone. She wasn't overly impressed with the transcript from my last school."

"You'll find that in her capacity as Duncan's mom she's a little nicer and wackier, if no less judgmental."

"So she won't tell me that another C-minus means community college, then an early pregnancy, then a series of unfulfilling hourly-wage retail jobs?"

"No, she won't tell you that stuff when she's at home. She'll still be *thinking* it, but she won't say it. Probably."

"Cool, then. I like Mr PiBB."

Jess and Syd marched out the side door of the garage, chitchatting. Stew simply glared at Duncan.

"Dude," he finally said.

"Dude what?" asked Duncan.

"Dude nothin'," said Stew. "Sometimes a situation is so fantastically messed up that all you can really say is 'Dude.'"

"So she's not a strong guitarist, I'll give you tha—"

"Not a strong guitarist?!" yelped Stew. "She's not any kind of guitarist, Duncan. I won't even say that she's a *bad* guitarist, because that would imply that she belongs to the global community of guitarists. Which she doesn't."

"Well, she looks cool," Duncan offered. "She's a punk rock girl who's not totally vulgar and covered in sores and eyebrow rings and stuff." He paused, running a finger over a dusty work surface, strewn with tools. "She has a tattoo," he added.

"I have a dim-witted cousin on my mom's side who has about a hundred tattoos. He's in a penitentiary in Oregon. He tried to rob a liquor store armed with a vacuum attachment. Can he be in the band? Did I mention he has tattoos?"

"Well, when he gets out, if he can play the bass, we might be in the mark—"

"Seriously, Duncan," said Stew. "She really sucked. I mean, nice girl. Don't get me wrong. Happy to know her, despite the fact that her brother's a raging psycho. But she just can't play. Not even a little."

"What can I do?"

"You can kick her out of the band is what you can do."

"Dude," he said, then fell silent.

"What?" asked Stew.

"This is one of those nothin'-to-say-except-'Dude' situations." Duncan, frustrated, sat on top of the dusty workbench. "I can't kick her out. She's Freddie's sister. I need Freddie. We have a deal. She's in the band, Stew. She's gotta be, or else I'm dead—either I'm metaphorically dead, or I'm physically dead. But dead."

"Then fix her."

"Wha—? You know she's not a puppy, right?"

"Make her better," said Stew. "At guitar. Make her suck less. *Way* less. She needs lessons, dude."

Duncan thought for a moment. Between band practices, homework, his dogged pursuit of Carly, and his burgeoning commitment to TARTS, he already felt a little overextended.

But he didn't want the band to completely stink, and he knew he'd been wildly inconsiderate to his friends. And anyway, Syd seemed nice enough. Perhaps this would earn him extra points with her brother.

"Okay," he said. "I'll try. It's kind of a delicate matter, though. One guitarist offering to give another lessons. But I'll pitch it."

"Cool," said Stew.

They heard voices and footsteps outside along the path that led to the garage.

"See, I told you Duncan's mom was a hoot," Jessie said to Syd as they returned. They were each carrying two Mr PiBBs. Jess tossed one to Stew, and Syd handed one to Duncan.

"Gross," said Stew. "Stuff tastes like liquefied dog hair."

"'Cuz you eat a lot of dog hair and you'd know?" asked Jess. "This stuff rocks."

"Thanks, Syd," said Duncan. "So, um . . . Stew and I were talking, Syd, and we thought maybe that you and I could sorta, um . . ." She looked at Duncan eagerly. He paused. "Well, we were thinking that you and I could play together a little bit. Just us. Ourselves. The guitarists. It's way important that we get the guitars to mesh. To interact. To develop an organic kind of relationship, an interplay, a unified—"

Syd snorted, then grinned. "You figured that since I totally *blow* you're gonna give me lessons, yeah?" She bounced in place. "Awesome! I totally need it. I suck. If you guys hadn't detected that, I would have lost all respect for . . . uh . . . what's the band's name, anyway?"

"Fat Barbie," said Stew.

"Awesome," said Syd. "Cool name. Total rejection of materialism. Nice."

"*Exactly*," said Duncan. "That's just what we were going for." He paused. "But, um . . . we've had a slight name modification." Stew and Jess glowered. "Very recently." More glowering. "Like, earlier today."

"But I was gonna get an overweight Barbie painted on the kick drum," said Jess. "Dang, Duncan!"

"Well, I'm sorry, it's just tha—"

"Oh, what's the friggin' name now?" asked Stew.

"The Flaming Tarts," Duncan offered with a hint of guilt.

"What?" asked Stew.

"Like Pop-Tarts?" asked Jess. "Like SweeTarts?"

"More like, um . . . Teens Against Rodent Tes—"

"No *way*!" yelled Stew. "You have *got* to be kidding me?! You are not gonna politicize this band, Duncan! No friggin' *way*!"

"You think naming the band after the little rat/beaver club is going to get you some sweet Carly lovin'?" asked Jess. "Is that what you think?"

Syd's eyes widened.

"Oh, just calm down," he said. "This doesn't make us political, exactly. We're only peripherally, um . . . less disconnected from the problems facing, um . . ."

"*Beavers!*" shouted Stew.

"The Flaming Tarts," said Syd. "I don't quite get it. Where are the beavers? And how is it political? Are Republicans setting beavers on fire and I've somehow missed this?"

"Well, it's complicated," said Duncan.

"It's lame," snapped Stew. "*L-a-m-e.*" He looked toward Jess. "Don't you have to get home? I'm definitely ready to go."

"Oh, yeah," she said, glancing at her digital watch. "Whoops. Later, um . . . Tarts. Nice to meet you, Syd!"

She and Stew grabbed their gear and hurried off, leaving Syd and Duncan alone in the garage. Duncan sighed and ran a hand through his hair.

"That could've gone better," he said.

"Lotta drama in this band," said Syd. "I think I'm gonna like it." She picked up her guitar. "So, how 'bout one of those lessons?"

Duncan sighed. "Yup. Sure. Gotta start sometime." He ripped off a quick sequence of notes.

"Hey, was that 'Witchcraft'?" she asked. "I love Wolfmother. Totally Sabbath-sounding, but still."

Point, Syd, thought Duncan. Yeah, this could all work out.

15

Or not. The first guitar lesson with Sydney Wambaugh addressed only the basics, and in a straightforward manner. She and Duncan reviewed guitar tablature, practiced chords, worked on transitions. "G, C, D," he said patiently. "Don't worry, you'll get it." She was determined, focused, and not easily frustrated. And she completely sucked.

Syd was miserably slow-fingered. Her hands seemed too tiny to control the guitar. It made wretched, horrible sounds. Duncan would have felt safer if he were giving her Uzi lessons. Outwardly, he tried to be encouraging. Inwardly, he was thinking of analogies to describe the terrible effect that her playing had on his senses: glass down a chalkboard, chewing tinfoil, removing his own fingernails with a grapefruit spoon—that sort of thing. Syd at least *looked* like a proper guitarist, he told himself. That was half the battle. Well, no. It was probably no more than 5 percent of the battle. But it was something. At six thirty, she put her guitar in its case and walked to the Monte Carlo.

"Very cool of you to try to help me, Duncan," she said. "As a musician, I know I'm not exactly Jimi Hendrix."

Dude, as a musician you're not exactly Jimmy Fallon, he thought.

"Oh, don't get down on yourself," he said. "That's the worst thing you can do. Think successful, be successful. That's what my Little League coach always told us."

"And did that work?"

"Not for baseball, no. Sure didn't. I can't hit speeding balls. It's my astigmatism. But I'm pretty sure the guitar is totally different." Syd smiled at that. "It's really just a matter of practicing. Come over on Thursday, same time. We'll try again." I'd seriously rather eat marbles, he thought. Big ones. But I owe Freddie.

"Cool," she said. "I'll be here." She smiled again. "'Bye."

"Hey, tell Freddie thanks."

Syd rolled her eyes, then got in the Monte Carlo and drove off.

Duncan locked up the garage and went inside the house. His mom commented on the fact that, for the second time in the past week, he'd worn an OWLS PHYS. ED. shirt home from school.

"Who does that?" she asked. "Are you trying to be ironic? Because if you are, we can buy you some nice-looking ironic T-shirts, honey. They have funny ones."

Duncan simply attributed the wearing of gym shirts to a newfound commitment to good health. "Healthy body, healthy mind, Mom. I'm taking control of my life. By God, I'm going to impress the President's Council on Physical Fitness." Then he grabbed a package of Twinkies and went to his room.

So you won't believe this, Mrs. K. (or maybe you will—hard to get a read on you), but here it is: today was another f*@#!ng awesome day. I really don't like to get all vulgar and explicit like that—it's not my nature. But sometimes a simple "awesome" or "great" or "sweet" just doesn't capture a moment. Such is the case again today. And I'm not just having manic mood swings consistent with general teenagedness. Overreactions, melodrama, blubbery gushing, etc. That's not my deal. I'm not prone to that, Mrs. K. No, I normally just find my level, like water, and I chill. But today with this girl (and I am officially divulging, for the record, that there is a girl at the root of all this emotionally charged good day/bad day jazz) was unreal—and I don't mean that in some smutty way, but in an emotional/intellectual way. (Oh, and she's hot, too. So there is that.) I'm way out of my league with this girl, Mrs. K.—waaaay out. In fact, I'm so far out of my league that I've had to lie to get in. But it's working, and it's hurting no one, so let's not dwell on the fine details of the courtship.

Arguably, the girl and I have a Jay Gatsby/Daisy Buchanan thing going on, but without the tragic closure (let's hope). And we have no past together.

And we're not really physically involved. And I'm not rich. But other than that, the comparison is solid. She's even got me thinking the H-word, Mrs. K.

That's right: Homecoming.

I've never been. I don't dance. That's why I play guitar. It's a thing to keep oneself occupied in lieu of dancing. But, well, homecoming is less than three weeks away. And I have a solid connection with this girl. I haven't breathed a word of this to anyone, though. It's for the best; things have a way of collapsing for me.

The band? Well, my progress with the girl has put a predictable strain on the band. There is a well-chronicled inverse relationship between romantic success and rock success. I'm living the classic arc: a world-changing band emerges; its songwriter meets a girl; the band implodes. Except for the world-changing and the implosion, that's another solid comparison right there. I've taken on a guitar protégée, too. A new kid in school, Syd Wambaugh. She is Earth's worst musician. I'll consider her training to be a stunning success if I can just help her to become, like, Earth's *second* worst musician. But that's a long way off.

Duncan put down the journal and ripped open the Twinkies. He reclined at his desk, his feet propped up. He held a Twinkie in his mouth like a cigar. For a moment he felt like a five-star general making tactical battlefield decisions that would affect the lives of countless others. But Duncan had played a lot of Risk as a kid and he knew, quite frankly, that it wasn't nearly so difficult to orchestrate a military campaign as it was to conduct a romantic campaign on multiple fronts. Woo Carly, get bullied, placate Freddie, infiltrate TARTS, teach Syd. Wash, rinse, repeat. The challenge ahead of him was monumental. It required cunning, deceptiveness, and intellect. He sighed, then bit off the end of the Twinkie and fished out some creamy filling with the tip of his tongue.

The sweet indulgence before the conflict, he thought.

In the days that followed, Duncan's various schemes unfolded with surgical precision, and they achieved precisely the desired results. He and Freddie conducted two more staged assaults that week—one of them a de-pantsing at Duncan's locker (he wore a flattering pair of flannel boxers for the occasion), and the other an elaborate after-school chase that ended with Duncan clinging to the crossbar of a goalpost. He and Freddie did a little bully/victim improv during gym, too. And Carly seemed enchanted by all of it. Freddie was absolutely brilliant, the perfect high school nemesis.

"We're an incredible team," Duncan told him privately. "Like Shaq and Wade. Or Kirk and Spock. Or Bobby and Whitney. Or Harold and Kumar. Or—"

"Shut up, dweeb."

"Will do."

Freddie's sister had another lesson. It was both fun and excruciating, which struck Duncan as very odd. He teased Syd for making crazed, primal guitar faces when she played.

"But those are my possessed-by-rock-and-roll faces. All great guitarists make faces. Otherwise you just look like a butcher or fry cook or bartender or something."

"The faces need to match the sounds, Syd. If you're not making the faces, maybe you could focus on, um . . . playing the right chords."

"I'd look like a chump."

"But you'd sound like a guitarist."

"Hmm. It's quite a choice, really."

Duncan noted that she looked pretty cool in her backward Minnesota Twins hat and her KISS T-shirt. If nothing else, she brought a cooler aesthetic and a classic rock posture to the Flaming Tarts. (And there really *was* nothing else.) He tried to teach her a fragment of "Louie, Louie." Syd somehow made it sound like "C Is for Cookie" from *Sesame Street*. Not just *kind of* like "C Is for Cookie," but *exactly* like it, almost note for note. Except with shrill, teeth-rattling feedback.

"It's really not that hard of a song," said Duncan, slightly exasperated but mostly amused.

"Yeah, I know," said Syd. "I've heard that before. It feels hard, though. All the moving my fingers around and everything. I have trouble with that."

"Should we try to find you a song where your fingers don't have to move?"

"Is there one?" she asked.

"No." He smiled. "But we could write one. It'd suck, though."

The time spent with Syd was fun but largely unproductive; the time Duncan spent with Carly, however, was spectacular on all fronts. He found that because most of his conversations with her dealt with things that were wholly contrived—his supposed fear of Freddie's attacks, his conversion to a rodent-saving zealot, his desire to assist with the upcoming TARTS rally—their interactions were unexpectedly effortless for him. He'd even developed a little confidence. Granted, it was confidence based on totally false pretenses. But hey, it was confidence nonetheless. Suddenly, Duncan could make her laugh. There was no more stammering, convulsing, or brain-farting when they were together. Increasingly, Carly seemed to view him as an interesting and relevant person, not simply as a victim in need of rescue. (Which isn't to say that Duncan was ready to stop playing the victim card.) He wasn't quite *comfortable* around Carly yet, but he knew what to do, when to do it, and how to spin it.

"You know, Duncan," she said to him over lunch, "I'm really glad I've gotten to know you—"

"Hey, me, too."

"—because TARTS needed fresh energy. You're so involved, so sincere."

"Yup," he said, "that's me. Involved. Sincere."

"The rally is going to be something truly special. I'm, like, tingly with excitement."

"Oh, so am I. Tingly."

"And I'm so stoked that the rally is on the same afternoon as homecoming. How perfect is *that*? It's going to get everybody talking about TARTS, Duncan."

"Everyone."

TARTS had begun to take up nearly all of Duncan's discretionary time. He arrived at school early to attend pre-rally briefings in Dr. Wiggins's classroom. He photocopied pro-rodent propaganda. He hung flyers about town, hitting the neighborhood near the college especially hard. He attended after-school meetings of the TARTS public relations subcommittee—and these didn't even involve Carly. Instead Marissa, a high-ranking handmaid, delegated various un-fun responsibilities to people other than herself, then she gossiped. But Duncan went to the meetings nonetheless. Doing so served both the near-term goal of taking Carly to homecoming and the long-term goal of having no fewer than fifteen children with her before he turned thirty. Duncan had burrowed so deeply into TARTS so quickly that he became, in a matter of mere days, an almost indispensable asset.

He also became somewhat distant from Jess and Stew.

"Dude!" called Jess, racing after Duncan down a hallway. "When are we gonna practice again?"

"Who?"

"Your *band*, assmaster! You, me, Stew, Syd . . . you do

remember us, right?" She swept in front of him to make eye contact. "Hello? Anyone in there?"

"Sorry, yeah." He stapled a TARTS leaflet to a bulletin board. "I'm just totally caught up in . . ."

"In not hanging out with your friends? Ever. Avoiding us like lepers. Not doing a thing to get us a friggin' gig. Generally not caring."

"I am not *avoiding* you." He sighed. "But I know. I've been busy. It sucks. I kinda suck. But I'm making real progress with Carly—and I've even written some new songs."

"Oh, let me guess. They're all about her." She sneered.

"No, for your information, they are *not* about her."

Jess stepped back. "Really? Not one? Hmm. What're you writing about, then?"

"Well, it's complicated." He looked away. "They're mostly unfinished songs."

"But the finished parts, what are they about?"

He fidgeted. "Um . . ."

"Well?" she said. "Don't be bashful."

"They're about test mice, mostly. But a couple of them deal more with rats."

Jess gave him a withering stare.

"They could be seen as metaphorical," he offered.

"You know that if we weren't at school—and I wasn't nearly finished serving about a month of detention—I'd kick you."

"I know that, yes."

"I still might."

"Please don't."

She shook her head disapprovingly. "Well, rat crusader, when can we practice? How 'bout tonight?"

"Tonight's no good, sorry. I'm giving Syd another lesson. It'll be the third this week—that's almost like having band practice."

"Except it's without half the band, dude." Jess folded her arms. "We've been hanging out a little, you know. Me and Syd. Since you began ignoring me. She's awesome. She was over on Wednesday. How's she progressing musically?"

"She's taken to guitar like the local Catholic Youth Ministry Club has taken to radical Islam."

"Oh."

"Yeah, she's not, um . . . competent. At all."

"Good thing we don't *actually* have any gigs, then. Can we practice Saturday afternoon, maybe?"

"I'll be at the mall."

"The *mall*? You're not a mall person, Duncan."

"I'm going for TARTS. They're gonna have a little booth or a kiosk or something. Like one of those places where they sell cubic zirconia jewelry or cheap hats. Except we're pushing the rodent-rights agenda." Jessie simply stared at him. He continued. "It's gonna be awesome. Carly is supposed be there in the morning, I think. And I agreed to be there all day. Well, at least as long as the mall is open."

Jessie walked away.

"Maybe we can practice on Sunday?" he said. "Jess?"

She waved her hand in obvious disgust.

16

Duncan arrived home after school on Friday exhausted but content. His dad's car was already in the driveway, which was highly unusual. Duncan walked through the front door, threw his backpack down near the stairs, and loped into the kitchen. His mom and dad were seated at the kitchen counter looking stiff and uncomfortable.

"Oh, man," said Duncan. "Did somebody die? It's not Aunt Dana, is it? That woman smokes like a facto—"

"No one died, Duncan," said his father. "And Dana's trying to cut back, she really is."

Duncan's mom gave his dad a moderately hostile look, then said, "We're not here to have the dangers-of-smoking discussion. We've already had that one."

"Um . . . then why are we here?" asked Duncan. "You're kinda freakin' me out."

"Pull up a stool, Duncan," said his dad, extending an arm.

"No way," Duncan said, shaking his head. "Not until you

tell me what this is all about. Am I being warned about something? Interrogated? Reprimanded? What?" His mind raced, trying to come up with something that might necessitate a confab with his parents. "And where's T?"

"Your sister is sleeping over at Emily's," said his mom in a too-calm voice.

"Whoa, you even made Talia clear out for this? What the heck? And why do you have to send her over to Emily's, that little ferret. Talia has lots of frie—"

"Duncan," said his father. "What's going on at school?"

There were many potential answers to that question: I'm kinda sorta lying to this incredibly sweet, incredibly hot girl, and she's diggin' me; I'm campaigning for better treatment for rodents, so rats and mice are diggin' me, too; I haven't understood a friggin' thing in Physics in over a week, so Dr. Wiggins is *not* diggin' me. But he likes the rodents. So maybe.

"Nothing," Duncan said defensively.

"Let me rephrase, then," said his father. "Is anyone bothering you at school?"

"Mom!" Duncan barked. "I can't *believe* you! Boundaries, Mom. You are not to use your position to intervene in my social affairs. It's like you've broken the fourth wall. We've talked about the fourth wall, Mom."

"This is a safety issue, Duncan," she huffed, "and I do not take it lightly." She looked at him compassionately. "What's the story with you and Freddie Wambaugh?" she asked.

I'm basically using him as a decoy to try to scam with the

aforementioned sweet, hot girl whom I've been lusting after for the past half decade, he thought.

"There is no story," he said. "None whatsoever. Are we done now?"

"No," said his dad.

"Duncan, I've heard a lot of tidbits over the past two years about you, your friends, your teachers—a lot. It's my job. I'm a guidance counselor, dear. I *guide*. And when you guide, you have to *know*. So I know things."

"Anytime you'd like to make sense, Mom, I'm listening."

Duncan's dad chuckled, which earned him a quick whack on the shoulder from Duncan's mom.

"Honey," she said, "several faculty members have come to me with reports of a boy—almost certainly *you*—who was chased across the football field and up a goalpost by Freddie."

Duncan said nothing.

"Is that accurate, honey?" asked his mother.

Duncan still said nothing. He merely frowned, then looked at his feet.

"I always hoped I'd see you in action on the football field, son," said his father. "I just never thought it would be cowering on a goalpost."

Duncan's mom administered another whack.

"You need to stand up to this boy, son," said his father. "Look, I know it's not easy, but you ca—"

"Oh, don't listen to your father, Duncan," said his mom. She glared. "At no point in his life would your father have stood up to Freddie Wambaugh. He's strong. And he's not one to back down from a confrontation—I've seen his disciplinary records." She looked toward Duncan. "We should talk to a dean, honey. Or I could talk to Principal Donovan for you. Or we could even call the Wambaughs and talk to the—"

"I can handle it," said Duncan.

"Oh now, honey, don't be like tha—"

"I can handle it, Mom," he said, almost pleading.

"Good man," said his father. "I'm glad we aired this out, talked it through." He made rapid, girlish punching gestures at the air. "It's important for families to talk about their problems."

"Can I *go*?" asked Duncan, definitely pleading.

"Sure thing," chirped his dad.

Duncan grabbed a Squirt from the fridge and began to walk toward the stairs.

"Honey," said his mom, "your father and I won't be home until late, okay?"

"'Kay," called Duncan. "Where're you going?"

"Oh, we're going to see Kenny Rogers at Pheasant Run," she said. "It was my birthday present, remember?" Duncan's dad began to sing "You Decorated My Life." Badly. (As if there were another way).

"How is it even possible that we share genetic material?" yelled Duncan, stomping upstairs. "The answer is that it's *not* possible. I am clearly adopted. I am the bastard son of Axl Rose."

He slammed the door to his room shut behind him, opened the Squirt, and turned on his laptop. He sat at his desk, fuming and scheming. Mom has no right to meddle in my non-academic school life, he told himself. But realistically he knew it was an inevitability. "Aaargh," he said aloud. "Duh." His head fell onto the desk. "Stupid, stupid, stupid."

His laptop beeped at him. Jess IMing, most likely. He pulled his head up and looked at the message.

UwereMeant4Me: Hey Dunky!

No idea who that is, he thought. Does anyone call me "Dunky"? Do I want to encourage this? Provocative screen name, though.

St4irw4y2Dunc4n: Who r u???

UwereMeant4Me: Carly! Hey! Got your IM info from your tarts app! Whassup!? ^_^

Duncan stared at the characters on his screen for a lost moment. Carly Garfield was IMing. That seemed so wildly beyond the limits of possibility that he couldn't process it as fact. Carly had only really known his name for, like, a week. And she'd only begun to take him seriously as a sentient human being, like, yesterday. Or possibly the day before. Whatever. And now she was IMing. Casually. With exclamation points and emoticons. He plugged his printer cable into a USB port—this exchange needed to be printed and scrap-booked. Not that he had a scrapbook. But he'd get one for something as momentous as this, his first IM from . . .

UwereMeant4Me: Dunky? U there?

Oh, crap, he thought. Stupid fingers . . . type something!

St4irw4y2Dunc4n: Hey Carly.

Ack, that was *stupid*. Be clever. And if you can't be clever, be nice.

St4irw4y2Dunc4n: Cool screen name. thought someone was
                        hitting on me.

UwereMeant4Me: LOL!

Why is that funny? She *might* hit on me, he thought. Someday. It's possible.

UwereMeant4Me: It's a Jewel song! She's AMAZING! I
                        (heart) Jewel!

Duncan's heart sank. This nugget of information totally blindsided him. Jewel was most definitely *not* on the Duncan Boone approved badass rocker list. She was, in fact, on the my-generation's-Cyndi-Lauper list. That was not a good list.

But fine, he thought. I just haven't had a chance to work on her music vocabulary yet.

> **St4irw4y2Dunc4n:** amazing. ;)
>
> **UwereMeant4Me:** Hey, just wanted u 2 know how gr8 it's been w/ tarts this week! U have been a >major< help! Thx!
>
> **St4irw4y2Dunc4n:** Least I could do. You've been saving me from Freddie all week. *shudder* Plus I'm totally into it. I kind of identify with the lab rat . . .

What a complete load, he thought. Was that maybe a little too thick? Hope she buys it.

> **UwereMeant4Me:** U r sooo sweet! :'(

Apparently, just thick enough.
Downstairs, the doorbell rang.

> **UwereMeant4Me:** I was excited 4 the rally be4 u joined tarts, but now I really can't w8! It's the biggest thing I've ever done! Happy 2 have u there!

"Duncan!" called his mom. "Oh, Duncan, you have a guest."

"Just a sec!" he yelled dismissively.

St4irw4y2Dunc4n: I'm excited too.

He heard footsteps on the stairs, as well as female voices.

UwereMeant4Me: Marissa and I have a >surprise< planned 4 the rally! Hope U like it . . . hope you'll join in! It should definitely get people's attention! ;)

St4irw4y2Dunc4n: *ph33r*

UwereMeant4Me: Hah! Don't be scared!

This was where he should make some sort of clever segue into a discussion of Carly's post-rally plans, he realized. An ideal opportunity to broach the topic of homecoming.

There was a knock at the door to Duncan's room.

"Duncan!" said his mom. "I said you have a guest." More knocking. "Can we come in?"

Flustered, he swiveled his head around and tapped a hand on his desk. This is just fate crapping all over me, he thought. A big stinking fate-dooky right on top of ol' Duncan Boone. Yup. Figures.

St4irw4y2Dunc4n: Later, Carly. Gotta run. Parent calling . . .

"Sure, Mom," he said. "C'mon in."

UwereMeant4Me: L8r Dunky! Bye!

His mother opened the door. Syd stood beside her, smiling a wry smile, a guitar case in her hand.

"It's none other than the delightful Sydney Wambaugh, honey," said his mom. "Freddie's sister." She stared at her son. "Isn't that something."

"She's with the band, Mom."

"Duncan's giving me lessons, Mrs. Boone," said Syd. "He's been a huge help with my fingering. I'm not really so good."

"I find this interesting on so many levels," said Duncan's mother, still staring at him. "But alas, I've got to go see Kenny." She hummed "You Needed Me" as she walked away.

Duncan and Syd stared at each other for an awkward moment.

"My mom has atrocious taste in music," he finally said. "In case you were wondering what your guidance counselor listens to when she's out power-walking. It's Kenny Rogers." He shivered. "Can you imagine?"

"Dinner music in my house is mostly AC/DC, Deep Purple—that sort of thing," said Syd. "My dad has a very narrow range of musical interests."

"Cool."

Syd peeped behind Duncan and saw the IM window.

"Oh, sorry," she said. "Don't let me interrupt. Chat away."

He spun back around and closed his laptop.

"No, no. Just this girl. It's actually the person who Freddie's helping me . . . um . . . it's complicated. And maybe not all that interesting to you."

"Was that Carly?" asked Syd. "*The* Carly?"

"Ah," said Duncan. "I see Jess has gotten to you."

"She might have mentioned that you had a special lady, yeah."

"She's not really . . . um . . . never mind." Duncan lowered his head.

Syd shifted slightly, scanning the walls of Duncan's room. Her eyes landed on a large poster composed of more than one hundred tiny square photographs, each of them a bit grainy, and several depicting something salacious, illegal, or both. Syd placed her guitar on the floor and walked over to the poster, which hung near the foot of Duncan's bed.

"Pretty sweet, eh?" he said. "Nobody fully appreciates it. At least not in my family. That's the original poster that came with the first pressing of—"

"—*A Nod Is As Good As a Wink* by the Faces," said Syd. "Came out in, like, seventy-one, right? And then they pulled the poster because everyone's parents were outraged. Totally rockin' album. Man, people should give the Faces their due."

Duncan was mildly stunned. "Well, I give 'em their due," he managed.

Syd leaned close to the poster, examining a square that featured a shirtless and heavy-lidded Rod Stewart. "Whoa, he was a hottie back in the day, eh?"

"Do you expect me to answer that?" said Duncan. "There's really no right answer for me here."

"Purely rhetorical," she said. "What the hell happened to Rod Stewart, anyway?"

"Disco, I think," said Duncan. "And then more recently, Rachel Hunter."

"That is so unfair," she snorted. "He happened to *her*, she did not happen to *him*. That dude started puttin' out crappy songs way before he met Rachel Hunter."

Duncan grinned. Syd propped a Doc Marten on the frame of his bed and ran her fingers over the edges of the poster.

"What are all these little orange pills?" she asked.

"I'm pretty sure they're vitamins," said Duncan. "To keep the band healthy despite the rigors of touring."

"*Riiight*," she said. "Are the Flaming Tarts this kind of band?"

"The kind that tours? No."

"I mean are we the kind that takes lewd photos of ourselves and our pills?"

"Well, we're evolving," said Duncan, leaning back. "It's too early to say. If we made a poster today, it'd probably be of me and Stew arguing while Jess tries to impale me with a drumstick. But you don't get posters if you don't get gigs. And the one consistent truth of this band is that we don't get gigs. But again, we're evolving."

Syd smiled. "Evolving takes time," she said. "Unless you have superpowered mutants!" She struck an action pose, legs splayed, karate hands extended.

Duncan snickered. "Do your mutant superpowers enable better guitar playing?" he asked.

"Sadly, no. So let's have another lesson."

17

So Syd had a guitar lesson. On Sunday she had another. And on Monday night, another. If the goal of these lessons had been to produce ultrasonic noises that repelled pests from the neighborhood, they could have been considered an overwhelming success. But that, of course, was not the goal. Syd was not improving. Her attempts at "Louie, Louie" were sounding less like "C Is for Cookie" and more like "Rubber Ducky," Duncan thought. This did not count as progress. He kept jamming with her because (1) despite sucking she seemed to be having fun, (2) she had impeccable taste and an encyclopedic familiarity with rock history, and (3) Duncan needed her in the band—'cuz of Freddie—and the band needed her to not suck if they were ever going to get a whiff of gig.

Meanwhile, the band was sick. Not literally, like with puke, but figuratively, like with dissension. Duncan had seen little of Stew and Jess since his immersion into TARTS. He'd been lunching exclusively with Carly at the TARTS table, convers-

ing (and flirting dorkily) with Carly between classes, and dart-
ing off to attend to pre-rally business before and after school.
Stew and Jess came to visit him at the mall kiosk on Saturday
afternoon. He was wearing a large button that featured a picture of an obese white rat with bloodred eyes.

"That's totally gross," said Jess. "That rat's the size of a
volleyball, dude."

"I think the idea is to gross you out," said Stew. "Sicken
the community until they commit to action."

"Something like that," said Duncan. "I think Carly said it's
a picture of a rat with a high trans-fat diet. Kinda like yours,
Jess."

"Then it will die content," she said.

Stew and Jess made Duncan commit to practicing on
Wednesday night—Jess even grabbed the pen from atop a
TARTS petition and wrote the time and date on Duncan's
forearm in blue ink:

F'ING TARTS! WED., OCT. 5, 4:45 PM! BE THERE
OR BE □!

"Just so you don't forget us."

"No-life club tonight?" asked Stew. "It's been a while."

"Actually," said Jess, "I'm supposed to go to an all-ages
show at Metro with Syd tonight. We hang out now. Because
all my other guitarist friends have abandoned me."

They left Duncan to his rat propaganda.

Wednesday arrived quickly. It was to be the band's first practice in over a week—it was the longest they had ever gone between practices since forming. It was also going to be the Flaming Tarts' first practice as a four-member unit. Duncan had been fake-bullied once more by Freddie on Tuesday, again resulting in the desired sympathy reaction from Carly—who this time biffed Freddie on the head repeatedly with a rolled-up TARTS sign—and his mom had again been informed by her anonymous faculty sources. Duncan decided that he could not control his parents' reaction to the bullying incidents, so he was going to try to push the issue far from his mind. Let 'em do what they're gonna do, he thought. He had enough to fret about already.

Like Syd's powerful vortex of guitar sucking, for example. Stew and Jess arrived at Duncan's garage ahead of her on after school on Wednesday. Stew demanded an update on her progress.

"The girl's had five lessons, Duncan. She must be a little bit better now, right? Otherwise your skills as an instructor must rival hers as a guitarist."

This is possible, Duncan thought. He certainly felt like he'd been telling Syd all the right things. And yet, well, she still made all those horrible noises.

"She's, um . . . I guess she's still kinda *raw* is what she is. Unfinished. But, y'know, I think she's getting it. Conceptually, if not, um . . . audibly. In any obvious way. Even a little. From what I can tell."

"So you're saying she has the *concept* down?" asked Stew.

"Yes, definitely."

"But her guitar still sounds like a rutting moose?"

"Basically, yes."

"Dammit, Duncan!" yelled Stew. "I thought I told you to fix her."

"She's not a lawn mower, dude. She's a suck-ass guitar player. It's different trying to fix those. Sometimes they never work."

"Then she shouldn't be in the friggin' band!" Stew insisted.

"Dude," said Duncan, "I think we all know why I need her in the band. That's the deal with Fred—"

"So *cancel* the deal with Freddie, Duncan!" yelled Stew. "You're already hangin' out with Carly every day, nonstop, all the effin' time. You've embedded yourself in the beaver brigade. She's not just gonna drop you."

"Well, she still sees me as kind of a reclamation project."

"So just tell Freddie that the deal's off because Syd's been kicked outta the band for gross incompetence. He'll still whup your ass—probably in an even more convincing manner—and Carly will still wanna save you. Or reclaim you. Or whatever she does to you." Stew angrily fussed with his bass, whipping open the lid of its case.

"But then Freddie might actually hurt me," said Duncan. "I need to keep this up at least until homecoming, if not longer."

"Are you actually taking Carly Garfield to homecoming?"

asked Jessie. "She doesn't seem like the school spirity, dance-attending type. Neither do you, Duncan."

"Well, it would be one of those hey-this-dance-is-coming-up-so-we-might-as-well-go type things," he said. "Elm Forest High School has provided the circumstances. So it's not like a *date* date. It's more like a matter of convenience. But I haven't asked her yet, no. And homecoming is the same day as this friggin' rally, so we'll see."

Stew seethed, snapping shut the lid of the case. "About Syd again," he said. "If she can't ju—"

"*Ahem!*" Jess cleared her throat loudly, cutting him off. "Syd's cool. Just thought I'd throw that out there. I mean, she's not so good at guitar. But she's very cool. She crowd-surfed at the Drunk Rhino show on Saturday. I think the band found her very amusing."

"So we'll make her a groupie," said Stew. "With full access. That's fine. But I don't see how we can have a band where one of the guitarists is just flat-out rotten."

"We could be a parody band," Duncan said, mostly joking.

"I don't find that funny," said Stew. He sat on the fender of his dad's car. "I thought the idea was to be a world-changing band with well-defined principles . . . pirate suits, stupid hats, et cetera." He sighed. "I used to totally love this band. Whatever we were named, and whatever we tried to play, I loved us. But now it's like we just exist so the lead singer can get hot chicks."

"Oh, that's so not fair," said Duncan, rolling his eyes.

"How is that not fair?" asked Stew.

"Sounds pretty accurate to me," added Jess.

"Well, for one thing it's not fair because I've been as dedicated to this band as anyone else—and you guys know that." Duncan stared at them. "And secondly, well . . . *all* bands exist so that the lead singer can get hot chicks. This band is no different. We're part of an ancient tradition."

They heard a heavy car door slam on the street out front.

"That'd be Syd," said Jess. "So can we table the discussion for a while?"

Stew stared at Duncan, who stared back.

"Cool heads, rockers," said Jessie. "Cool heads. Let's just relax."

Seconds later, Syd entered the garage in a rush. "Hey!" she said happily. "This is so exciting—the whole band together, finally." She opened her guitar case, then fist-bumped Jessie. "Maybe all I needed were a few more instruments to drown me out, eh, Duncan?" She snorted. "Sorry if I'm late, by the way. Had to drop Freddie off at work."

"He works?" asked Duncan. "Like, for an employer?"

"Freddie? Hell, yeah. Works like a sled dog, actually. Keeps him in that piss-poor mood all the time." She looped the guitar strap over her head. "So are we gonna try one of the new songs, Duncan?"

"The 'new' songs?" asked Stew with a smirk.

"Oh, um . . ." Duncan shifted nervously.

"C'mon, dude!" urged Syd. "They're not bad at all. Kind of a new genre for the Tarts, from what I understand."

"A new genre!" said Stew with feigned enthusiasm. "Sounds fantastic. What genre are we exploring, Duncan?"

"Well, I don't know that it can be easily classified, really. A genre is really just a label, after all, and this band doesn't really do labels, so . . ."

"How 'bout if you had to give the genre a name. What would it be?"

"Um . . . *rodent*, I guess. If I had to name it." Duncan shifted uncomfortably.

Stew glared for a moment. "You are such a weenie, Duncan," he said, then turned toward Jessie. "Did you know about this?"

"Duncan might have mentioned something. I didn't realize he'd actually worked out the instrumentation."

"And you're okay with this?" Stew asked.

Jessie seemed taken aback. "Uh . . . well . . ."

"Hey, there are a lot of kick-ass songs about rodents," offered Syd. "This is not uncharted musical territory."

"Like what?" asked Stew.

"There's 'Rat Salad,' by Sabbath."

"Doesn't count," said Stew. "That's an instrumental."

"Well," she continued, "There's 'Muskrat Love.' Is the muskrat a rodent?"

"America sings it," said Duncan, smiling. "And yes, definitely a rodent."

"There's also 'Street Rats' by Ted Nugent," said Syd. "And 'Rat Trap' by the Boomtown Rats, and 'Rodent' by Skinny Puppy, and 'Rats' by Sonic Youth. Oh, and there's 'Fox Squirrel' by Muddy Waters—I'm pretty sure that either foxes or squir-rels are rodents. I'm not sure which is what. And there's—"

"But are any of those songs actually *about* rodents?" said Stew. "Like, are they about saving rodents from the perilous conditions in laboratories, or whatever Duncan's writing about?"

Syd shrugged her shoulders and began to reply, but Stew cut her off.

"No," he said. "In a word, *no*. They are not. Duncan is working alone in the rodent genre. He is a pioneer."

"There's that one Primus song," offered Duncan. "'Wyno-na's Big Brown Beaver.' That's definitely about, um . . . a bea-ver." He smiled. "Which we've established is a rodent."

"Oh, and I suppose you've been writing songs just like that one, have you?"

"Well, no. Not *just* like that. I don't think that Carly would quite see the humor in a song abou—"

"See, *that's* the problem!" said Stew. "Everything we do—everything *you* do, Duncan—is totally about that tart!"

Syd snorted again. "Sorry," she said. "It's just, well . . . 'tart.' That's funny. TARTS, tart. She's a tart. Heh."

Stew stared. "Let's play something," he said flatly.

"How 'bout one of the older songs?" said Duncan.

"From the pre-Blowhole days," said Jessie.

"Our first song," suggested Duncan. "'Mr. Trampoline Man.' It starts with that wicked bass line, Stew. C'mon . . .'"

"Okay, fine." Stew didn't quite smile.

He's not usually this high-maintenance, thought Duncan.

The band ripped through three songs, hardly pausing for

breath between them. Syd sat off to the side, listening, grinning, and nodding her head. From Stew's opening notes to Jessie's atomic drum finale, the mini-set lasted no more than seven minutes. When they were finished, Duncan's chest was heaving and all three were soaked in sweat.

"That," said Syd, "was awesome." She clapped, then hopped in place enthusiastically.

"Okay, *chica*," said Jessie, "now you've gotta play a little something." She wiped perspiration from her forehead with the back of her hand.

"Sweet!" said Syd. She struck a very classic guitar pose, her feet slightly apart, her hands ready, and the neck of the guitar angled slightly upward. "Let's all just remember I suck," she said.

"Oh, that's right," said Stew. "I'd totally forgotten."

"Back off, dude," said Duncan, growing testy. "We're in my garage. In the suburbs. With no one around. At all. Just us. She's welcome to suck here—anyone's welcome to suck here."

"Well have at it, then," said Stew. "Suck away."

Duncan looked at his small protégée. She had the Twins cap on again, this time twisted to the side, and an oversize Trip Shakespeare shirt. Her tiny hands twitched on the guitar strings. She had a determined, don't-F-with-me expression on her face. She glared at Stew, then looked toward Duncan as if for help.

"We'll try 'Mousey, Mousey,' Okay?" He glanced at Stew and Jessie. "It's just basically 'Louie, Louie' with, um . . . well, with 'Mousey,' not 'Louie.'"

"'Cuz TARTS," said Stew.

"Yes," said Duncan. "That's correct, Stew. 'Cuz TARTS. There are a few rodent-related lyrical twists, but not many."

Jessie laughed. Stew shook his head in disgust. Duncan looked into Syd's eyes.

"You can do this," he said.

You stink at this, he thought.

"Okay," she said. "I'm ready."

No, really, he thought. You stink.

"The chords are simple," he said. "A, D, E-minor. Simple."

"Got it," said Syd. "Let's rock."

"All right," said Duncan. "On my count." He paused. "One, two . . . a-one, two—"

"You might wanna plug that thing in," said Stew, gesturing at Syd's guitar.

"Oh, right," she said. "Heh." She plugged into an amp, snorted again, then restruck the guitar pose. "Ready," she said.

The song lasted exactly thirteen seconds. In that time, Syd seemed to battle her guitar like it was a vicious reptile that had clamped onto her abdomen and wouldn't let go. She sent a shriek of feedback into the air, followed by a sequence of atonal *pwangs*, and then she broke two strings. The band—and Syd—stopped playing.

"Whoops," she said, apparently unbowed. "Heh." She touched the limp ends of the broken strings. "I've got more in the car. Be right back."

She leaned the guitar against a wooden shelf. It remained there briefly, then fell to the floor when Syd threw open the garage door. "Whoops," she said again, then scampered out to her Monte Carlo.

"Dude, how many gigs did we play before Freddie's sister joined the band?" asked Stew, staring at Duncan.

"None," he answered. "I think we all know tha—"

"And how many do you think we're gonna play now that our rhythm guitarist is a ninety-pound piece of pure *sucktastic suckiness*?!"

"Hey, Stew," said Duncan. "She's a total beginner, man. She'll get bet—"

"Oh, don't tell me she'll get *better*. I thought the idea was that this band—the three of us—would get better, write songs, get gigs, produce a couple of critically acclaimed indie releases, then sign with, like, Sony BMG for a zillion dollars and buy a plane." He paused. "Well, wasn't that the plan?"

Jessie tried to calm him. "Syd's cool, Stew. She just nee—"

"I don't care that she's a cool chick! She's not helping this band. All she's doing is helping Duncan get some hot loony chick." He gently put his bass down. "I can't handle this. She's seriously gotta go, Duncan."

"I can't kick her out of the band, Stew. Not *now*."

"Then I'm gone," he said. He hurriedly packed his bass and brushed past Duncan. "Done. As in, I quit." He wiped his hands together slowly, as if scraping the crumbs of the Flaming Tarts from his fingers.

"Stew," said Jessie, "I drove you here, remember? You can't just—"

"I'll walk home."

"That's like seven miles, dude. And you have to cross two expressways."

"So drive me."

Syd skipped back into the garage. "What's up?" she said cheerily. "We're not done already, are we?"

"Oh, we're beyond done," said Stew. "We're history." He walked outside.

Jessie followed. "Sorry, dude," she whispered to Syd.

Duncan slumped forward, resting both hands on his dad's car.

"What just happened?" asked Syd.

But Duncan remained silent. Unbelievable, he thought. No band, no Freddie. No Freddie, no Carly. No Carly . . . no point.

"Seriously, Duncan, what just happened? Was there a fight? Did you get hit with stuff again? Are you wounded?"

"Wounded," he said quietly. "A little. There was a minor fight, yes. No instruments were thrown. I think we're . . . um . . . not a band anymore."

Syd stood glumly for a moment, absently twisting the Twins hat around her head. "Guess the lessons are over."

Duncan couldn't answer. He leaned on the car, his head buried in his arms.

18

Leaning back against his locker amid the pre-class morning buzz of students, Duncan yawned, then bent his knees and slid to the floor. His eyes drooped. His mouth drooped. He drooped. At most he'd slept two hours the night before. The breakup of the Flaming Tarts had crushed him. He thought about writing in his English journal, then realized that Mrs. Kindler had collected all the journals the previous Friday. Next he thought about writing melancholy song lyrics. But of course he no longer had a band. So what was the point?

No point, he decided.

The words repeated in his head: No band, no Freddie. No Freddie, no Carly. No Carly, no point. He sighed, then yawned again. A wadded-up piece of notebook paper hit him in the face.

"Hey, rocker," said Jessie. "Well, *ex*-rocker."

"Don't joke," said Duncan. "There is no humor here."

"Where's your girl? Your honey? Your baby? Your pooh? Your swee—"

"Another TARTS meeting."

Jessie snickered. "It sounds like that dorky card game. TARTS: The Gathering."

"The joking. Make it stop. Hurting."

"So you're taking the band's breakup well, I see."

He said nothing.

"Duncan, if it's really meant to be, then—"

"—then I'll find a way to mess it up. To kill it dead. To eviscerate it. I will find a way to single-handedly ruin it—whatever it is—if it's meant to be." He yawned again. "Is that what you were gonna say?"

Jessie stared at him for a moment. He continued drooping.

"Okay," she said. "Well, I think we both know that I am not the kiss-it-make-it-better type of girl. So I'll be going." She walked away air-drumming.

Duncan yawned again.

Minutes passed. First bell neared. Carly returned. "Hey, Dunky," she said. "You missed the meeting."

"Yeah, I . . ."

"It's okay," she said. "I realized you were probably posting signs for the rally like we'd talked about." She patted his head as though he were a sheepdog. Carly fussed with the contents of her locker, withdrawing a few books. "I can't believe things are coming together so well. Everything is just . . ."

She searched.

". . . well, it's perfect," she finally said, then bounded off.

Duncan sat, his legs now extended along the floor, his back pressed against the locker. More yawning. The bell rang. He kept sitting, only rising and walking to class when the halls were nearly empty.

He trudged wearily through the day, saying little and doing less. He noted that he, Stew, and Jess all sat at different lunch tables. Duncan, of course, sat with the TARTS. Stew sat by himself. Jessie sat with Syd, and the two of them appeared to be engaged in a rather intense discussion.

Bet she went straight home and told her brother about the band, Duncan thought. Damn, damn, damn.

Freddie sat alone at his usual table, the one he'd pillaged from the conquered Goths. When would he attack? wondered Duncan. It was coming—that much was certain.

Mrs. Kindler seemed to take a special interest in Duncan that afternoon, attempting at several points to rouse him to discuss plot points of *Gatsby* in class. This irritated him to no end. He felt he was emitting the strongest possible don't-call-on-me-I'm-depressed vibe, and he wanted Mrs. Kindler to respect it. Honor the vibe, he thought. She didn't.

"Duncan," she said, creeping toward his desk. "What do you think about the relationship in the novel between the *illusory* and the *real*?"

No you didn't, Mrs. K., he thought.

"We want the illusion," he said.

She stared at him, raising her eyebrows in a not-so-subtle gesture that said "keep talking." He did, but his heart certainly wasn't invested in the response. And he resented having to answer any question at all, given his evident misery.

"They do. In *Gatsby*, the characters. They're after illusions, to the exclusion of whatever's real. They're all façade. The money, the affairs—which we mostly just hear about and rarely see, which stinks—" Muted laughter from the class. "—there isn't much that's real at all. At least nothing outward." He prattled on as Mrs. Kindler nodded.

She had posed the last intellectual challenge of his school day. Duncan navigated the remainder of his schedule quietly. Having nothing better to do after school—what with no band practice and no guitar lesson to get home to—he attended Marissa's TARTS committee meeting. Predictably, it sucked. He nearly slept, but was jarred awake when Marissa began making derisive, catty cracks about Carly. At this, he stood and left, his backpack slung over his sagging shoulder.

Duncan walked slowly toward his car, alone. The late-afternoon October air was crisp and the sky a tinny gray. Leaves fell and drifted. With his head down and his eyes half-closed, he was fumbling with his keys at the door of his Reliant before he noticed Freddie seated on the trunk. And he sure looked pissed.

"Duncan, Duncan, Duncan," he said, shaking his head and punching a meaty hand against a meaty palm. For an instant, Duncan considered running. He felt an adrenaline surge, but gloom and inevitability beat it down. He merely sighed, and a confession came rushing out.

"Look," said Duncan flatly. "It's not my fault. Well, okay, it's partly my fault in a technical sense—if we're attributing blame—but it's not like I didn't try. I *did* try, Freddie. I tried hard. I mean, you know how many guitar lessons I've given Sydney, right? A lot. More than I'd expected to when we struck this little accord, that's for damn sure. I want her to be a great guitar player. I really do. Heck, I'd settle for Syd being just a bad-but-serviceable guitar player. But she isn't, dude." Duncan held up his hands. "She just isn't. She stinks, man. She's *dangerously* bad. The sounds she makes, they're awful. Like big screechy science fiction noises. She cannot play guitar out loud for a band that wants to entertain people. She just sucks, dude. And it broke the Flaming Tarts apart." Duncan sighed again. "You should've seen Stew last night. I really thought he was gonna go nuts, throw stuff and get all Freddie Wamba—"

He paused.

"Okay, bad choice of words there. Sorry. Anyway, Stew was pretty mad. The band is broken up, and I can't just pull it back together. If I could, I would. But the way things ended . . . I just don't know how to fix it, Freddie. I can't make Sydney a virtuoso overnight—and even if I could, I don't know if I could get Stew back. And without a bass guitar, we don't really have a band, do we?"

Freddie stared at him. His eyes had narrowed, as if he were trying to make out a distant object. After several seconds he spoke. "What the hell are you talking about, dipweed?"

Duncan returned a perplexed expression. "I'm talking about the band breaking up, dude. Your sister coming home last night, probably pissed at me. No more Flaming Tarts . . . does that ring a bell?"

"Nope," said a plainly confused Freddie. "I was just gonna give you crap for getting me suspended."

"*What?!*" said Duncan. "Suspended? I didn't get you *suspended*. I need you at school, bullying."

"Well, you're not gonna get it. Not for the next five school days, anyway. I am officially suspended, effective immediately. Multiple violations of the district's code of student conduct blah-blah-blah. I'm not supposed to be on school property at all, actually. So I'm risking further discipline by being here in the parking lot talking to you, doofus."

"But I didn't complain to anyone! This is *definitely* not my fault, Freddie. You're no good to me at home. You've gotta kick my ass, dude. We have a special dynamic. I can't believe this is happening to me."

"Actually, it's happening to me," said Freddie. "Are you *sure* that you never complained to any faculty or staff member? You're positive? You never mentioned me? Not to anyone?"

"Hell, no. Why would I—?" He paused. "Oh." Duncan leaned forward onto the roof of the car. "I suppose my mom might have had something to do with this."

"Bingo," said Freddie. "In fact, the Assistant Dean of Students who sentenced me made a special point of telling me that the next time I single out a student to torture, I shouldn't pick the child of a guidance counselor." Freddie chuckled. "I told him that if Chambliss had a kid, that's definitely who I'd torture."

"What if I go to Principal Donovan and explain every-thing—and I do mean *everything*, Freddie. I'll do it. I feel lousy that you're in this mess. A suspension is kind of a big deal."

"Look, dorkstick, if you do anything to screw up this sus-pension for me, I *will* kick your ass. They've handed me five vacation days, and I'm takin' 'em. It's not like my permanent record can get any uglier. This may be the first time I've been suspended by *this* school, but it's not exactly the first time I've been suspended by *a* school. They still have wanted posters of me in Bemidji, I'm pretty sure."

"So is there anything I can do? Talk to your parents on your behalf? Bake you a cake with a file in it?"

Freddie laughed an easy laugh. Suspension seemed to suit him. "My mom and dad are not disturbed by my rule-breaking. Don't sweat it, dweeb. But there is something I need you to do."

"What is it? I'll do it. No problem, man. Anything."

"I'd like a girl."

They looked at each other for a moment.

"I don't get it," said Duncan. "You want what?"

"What's not to get? I'd like a girl."

"You mean like I should pretend to bully *you* for a while so that some girl will come to your defense and—"

"No, dork. I mean like you set me up. With a girl."

"Hell, Freddie, you've got a job. You've got money. I've heard that for, like, fifty bucks you can go to North Avenue and there's a whole bunch of girls in spandex dres—"

"Dude!" said Freddie, clearly insulted. "What do I look like, a total scuzz?"

Yes, thought Duncan. Like scuzziness personified.

"No. I just . . . well, I'm not quite following you here. You want a girl? For what purpose?"

"'For what purpose?'" repeated Freddie. "For the same reason you wanna get with that beaver chick."

"Okay, why is it that everyone has to make the beaver cracks? It's impolite. She's protecting rodents—all rodents."

"Whatever, dweeb. I wanna meet a girl to, like, hang out with. To do stuff with. To converse with—like about my life, school, chasing dorks. Typical boy/girl stuff."

Don't you get soft on me, thought Duncan. Don't do it. Not you, Freddie.

"You mean like you want a companion?"

"If by 'companion' you mean 'attractive female companion,' yeah. The assistant dean was telling me today that my suspension ended just in time for homecoming—and then the smug poopsniffer *laughed*. Can you believe that? He laughs at my romantic prospects. I'll admit that I may not have traditional manners and good looks"—he scratched the folds of his beefy neck—"but I can turn up the charm. And I'd like a homecoming date."

"A homecoming date," said Duncan. "Hmm." I'd actually like one of those, too, he thought. "What made you come to me with this request, Freddie? Just out of curiosity. I mean, if I were any good at talking to girls, I would never have needed you."

"You're a smart kid, dorkmonkey. I like the way you've played things with the rodent chick. Plus, let's face it, I have all kinds of leverage with you." Freddie did the punch-his-palm thing again. "Find me a girl. A date. For homecoming." He cracked his neck. "Or you'll get the 'Freddie Special.'"

That seemed bad.

"Okay," said Duncan. "I'll try."

"Don't try. Do it. You've got five days."

Freddie began to walk away. After several steps, he turned around. "Syd is really that bad? Seriously?"

"It's like listening to orangutans whack each other with live monkeys."

Freddie raised his eyebrows. "That's a graphic description."

"I've had a *lot* of time to consider Syd's guitar playing."

19

"I've hit a wall," said Duncan, plopping himself down next to Jessie at lunch on Friday. "An impossibly large wall. Like with concrete and steel and razor wire."

"Oh, I'm sorry," Jessie said in a fairly hostile tone. "I didn't realize I'd sat down at the Flakeballs Against Rat Test Stuff table. I'll move."

Duncan laughed quietly.

"I'm insulting you, Duncan," she said.

"Funny acronym. FARTS. Flakes Against da-da-da-da."

Jessie smiled. "Okay, so I'm amusing even when I'm trying to be bitter and spiteful. *That's* when you know you're an adorable person." She bit into a celery stick. "What have I done to earn your lunchtime presence?"

"You don't eat celery. What are you doing?"

"I'm watching calories. Keeping slim and fit."

"You *what*?"

"The big dance is coming up. Homecoming. Our beloved Owls taking on . . . hmm, I believe it's the Bulldogs."

"You don't dance. You're a drummer."

"I'm a little bit of a babe, it turns out. I have a date."

"A date? Like, with destiny?"

"No, a boy human."

"Who asked you?"

"It's who I asked. Wake up to the new millennium, Fonzie."

"So who'd you ask, tramp?"

"Sloth."

Duncan laughed again. "Good one. Sloth."

"No, really. Sloth. I called him."

"Come *on*. No you didn't. I mean, a nice guy, Sloth. But you were attracted to hi—"

"Oh, ick. No." She chomped another celery stick. "I'll admit that I kinda like the bad boys. But not the furry bad boys. No, I just thought he was a nice guy. And it seemed kind of sad, Sloth workin' the third shift just to afford a dinky bugtrap in that war-zone apartment complex. He's had no authentic high school experiences. Zero. None. A Maple North outlaw. Kinda sad. So, after you and I blatantly misjudged him, I thought it would be a nice gesture to take him to a function. And he can't really go to one of his own school's events, what with his reputation. So he's coming to one of ours."

Duncan stared, slightly bewildered. "That's so . . . hmm, there's a word . . ."

"Nice? I know. I am nice to a fault. I am kindness itself."

"Something like that, yeah. It is nice."

"Celery?" she said, offering a stick from her pile.

"No thanks."

"These things suck. Like eating fingers. I don't know how anorexics do it—the broth, the carrots, the lettuce, the fasting. Gimme a stack of cookies, yo." She chewed, looking miserable. "So why are you visiting the old lunch table? Feeling nostalgic? There was something about a wall, right?"

"Yes, the wall. I've hit it. That's what I said before you dropped this Sloth bombshell."

"What the hell does that mean, 'hit the wall'? Isn't that a sports analogy? Please don't use those." She bit into more celery.

"Sorry. I'm just stressed. Nearing a breakdown, maybe. There's the demise of the band. Stew hates me. I'm neck-deep in TARTS responsibilities—and I hate, hate, *hate* rats, by the way." He sighed. "And there's this ongoing lie with Carly, which I'm feeling horrible about because one, it's a lie, and two, it got Freddie suspended. Or my mom got him suspended because of the lie. But whatever." He thought for a moment. "Oh, and get this: I have to find Freddie a date for homecoming. Why didn't you tell me you had a thing for goons before today? Where was this information being kept?"

"You don't really ask what other people are thinking, Duncan. At least not lately."

He looked down. "Sorry. I know. So what *are* you thinking?"

"I'm thinking that Stew doesn't hate you. He just thinks you've prioritized a stupid fantasy over your friends, which you have. And I'm thinking that I can work with Freddie a little to get him date-ready." She spit a wad of partially chewed celery onto her tray. "*Blech*. Seriously, these things are vile. I especially hate the ends. It's like gnawing on cold wool." She took a sip of her soda. "Lastly, I'm thinking that Syd's going to be sitting here in about a minute, and you should apologize to her."

"For what?"

"For making her feel like she's responsible for breaking up the band. For making her feel like a complete failure."

"But she's responsible for breaking up the band. And she's a complete failure."

"You can be such a jackass, Duncan."

He heard sniffling from over his right shoulder and the approach of Birkenstocks. He saw Jessie looking up at someone behind him, so he turned. Carly stood there, teardrops running down her cheeks. She sniffled again, then produced a loud, emotive "*Ohhhhh . . .*"

"Carly!" he said, standing and offering her a seat. "What is it? What's wrong?"

She sat next to him, continuing the audible crying. He'd had never seen her so distraught. He'd seen her cheerful, amused, and aggressive—but never sad. Not like this. Like, with sobbing and mucus and goo and tears. She sat, then fell against his shoulder, closed her eyes, and cried louder. Jess looked at him coolly and made a gagging motion with her finger.

"Oh, Duncan," sobbed Carly. "It's so awful." More tears. "I don't know what I'm going to do. . . ." Sniffle, sniffle.

Jess tilted her head, pointed at Duncan, and made a talking gesture with her hand. He knew he should say *something*, but he wasn't prepared to comfort Carly—his more successful interactions with her required preparation. But he tried.

"W-what's up, Carly?" he said hesitantly.

Great, he thought. Whassup? Idiot. Like you just greeted her at Applebee's.

"Oh, Duncan! It's terrible. Terrible! The TARTS rally is . . . [*sniff*] completely falling apart! It's awful!" She sobbed against his arm.

Jessie rolled her eyes.

"What happened?" Duncan asked. "How can it fall apart? Things can't be so bad. We plan every day. We double-check, we triple-check. We've plastered the town in flyers. We're like an elite paramilitary group. We—"

"The band!" Carly sobbed. "We lost the band! And the rapper! They were like . . . [*sniff*] a package deal. Tripbunny and . . . [*sniff*] MC Fatso. I was *so* excited, too. I was [*sniff*] . . . so counting on this. The band was going to . . . [*sniff*] be this big crescendo for the rally. All these VIPs from the national . . . [*sniff*] TARTS organization are coming into town. And we *promised* . . . [*sniff*] live music! It's on the posters, Duncan!" More sobbing. "The posters . . ."

Duncan looked at Jessie. She raised her hands as if to say, *I have no part in this, dude.* Duncan flashed her a thumbs-up. Carly sniffled loudly on his arm. Jessie gave him a look that seemed to ask, *How is this good?*

"Relax, Carly," said Duncan. "It's okay. My band will play the rally."

Carly stiffened, giving Duncan a quizzical look. Jessie gave him a significantly more quizzical look.

"Are you guys, um . . . good?" asked Carly.

Jessie leaned forward across the table. "Hey, dude, we don't eve—"

"We *rock*," said Duncan firmly. "I mean, unless you want us to slow it down. 'Cuz we can do that, too. We can do whatever's needed, basically. We're a versatile band. And very socially conscious. We've actually been looking to do, you know, um . . . more rallies and benefits and such."

Jessie's mouth fell open. Duncan continued.

"We've been together a long time, Carly. We pretty much rock." He looked into her eyes. "Really." He looked at Jessie, who seemed astonished. "We don't have any other gigs next Friday, right?"

"Nope," she said, shaking her head, her eyes wide. "Not a single one."

Carly brightened. She wiped her eyes, then enveloped Duncan in a hug. He flashed Jessie another thumbs-up. Syd arrived at the lunch table looking mortified.

"Oh, Duncan, I am soooo grateful!" said Carly. "You are a total savior. Where have you been my whole life?"

Stalking you mostly, he thought.

"It's nothing," he said.

She took his face in her hands and planted a kiss on his

cheek. He blushed. Carly then leaned back and gave him a sly smile. "Okay, I *have* to tell you how the rally is ending," she said. "Because the band is key. I can't even contain myself." Her knees bounced excitedly. "So all the speakers will have spoken—a city councilwoman, a state legislator, the morning deejay from XRT, me—of course—and I introduce . . . what's your band's name again?"

"The Flaming Tarts," said Duncan, smiling, pleased with himself.

"The Tarts!" said Carly. She squeezed him again. Jessie and Syd exchanged a look. "So I'll introduce the Flaming Tarts," continued Carly, "and you'll come out and play for, like, fifteen minutes—no explicit lyrics, please, we're at the park—and then . . . *oooh*, this is so great! The girls and I—everyone: Kylie, Hayley, Marissa, Zoe, Chloe, Sophie—we streak across the park with this giant banner."

She looked at Duncan for a reaction.

"That's cool," he said. "I like banners."

"Duncan, we *streak*."

"Like you have a race?"

"Like we're naked. Stripped, just like rats are stripped of their rights."

Syd snorted. Jessie half spewed soda on her tray. Duncan merely stared, imagining the scene. It was not unpleasant.

"The hope," said Carly, "is that we all get arrested or something. That'll get TARTS *so* much attention. We know the Elm Forest police will be there, so there's a decent chance."

Duncan kept staring. "What, um . . . what gave you this idea, Carly?" he finally asked.

"Well, you know how we've been calling TV stations trying to get someone to cover the rally? No one was interested. No one at all. But then Kylie and I were downtown last weekend and we sort of forced a Fox News van off the road. We made our pitch about the rally—right on the side of Lake Shore Drive, cars and trucks whizzing past—and this producer was all like, 'What's the hook?' And we're like, 'Hook?' And he's saying, 'This is Chicago. There are rallies. Big whoop. Will there be a million people? Will there be violence? Is anyone naked?' And I was like, 'Deal. We're *so* naked.' And he was like, 'Can we have an exclusive?' And I was like, 'Yes!' So we streak."

"You're getting naked?" Duncan said. "Definitely? And risking arrest?"

"Definitely."

"We're proud to be your band," he said.

Carly winked at him and said, "I'm glad you're going to be there, Duncan. It's going to be an awesome day." She stood, dabbed tears from her cheeks, and began to walk away. Then she turned her head back, grinning. "Hopefully it'll be a great night, too."

Duncan stared at Jessie, a stunned expression on his face. "What did that mean? 'A great night'? That's good, right?"

The phrase had galactic heft. It overwhelmed Duncan. "A great night." Vague, he thought, yet still somehow an explicit promise. Carly *had* to know how Duncan would define "great night." Was she acknowledging some shared sense of romantic inter—?

"Dude!" interrupted Jess. "You have a minor problem. There is no band. I mean, I'll play. As long as Syd is in." Jessie elbowed Sydney. "But Stew? Man, Stew's pissed."

Without a word, Duncan walked to where Stew sat, alone and sullen, in a far corner of the cafeteria.

"I apologize," he said. "Wholeheartedly and without reservation. Now come on, get up. We have to go sit with Jess and Syd. We need to come up with a set list. The band is back together."

Stew stared with a severe expression. "You think you can walk over here, wave the magic apology, and—*poof!*—I'm back in the band? Well, you can't. There is literally *nothing* you could say that would make me reunite with the band. Nothing."

Duncan stood unmoving, eyeing him for a moment. "We have a gig. There will be at least seven naked women there."

Stew blinked. Then he stood, picking up his tray. "Okay, well, I can practice pretty much any night, any time. We should definitely work through some of the new rodent material, I guess. . . ."

20

Band practices resumed with renewed vigor: two and a half hours on Friday night, three hours on Saturday. Duncan allowed all his other responsibilities—most notably finding Freddie a date—to fall by the wayside. The Flaming Tarts convened again on Sunday afternoon, and they vowed to keep jamming until they'd perfected a six-song set. For the good of the group and the promise of rampant nakedness, Stew showed remarkable patience with Syd. She, however, did not display any improvement on guitar whatsoever. But when frustration crept over Duncan, he repeated three words to himself like a mantra: "A great night." It centered him. Syd would become competent, he vowed. And she was trying extremely hard—that much was clear. Duncan rewrote much of the new rodent-related material, simplifying Syd's responsibilities to a ludicrous extent. But somehow she was always just . . . off.

"Potty break!" called Jessie.

"Dude," said Duncan, "we're still totally struggling with the bridge on 'Mouse of Pain.' Just one more time through, okay?"

"I *said* potty break," Jessie insisted, standing up and walking toward the door. "My drumming does not improve when I have to pee. I just get faster."

Duncan sighed. Stew set down his bass and walked toward the door, too.

"I'll jump on the potty wagon," he said.

Soon, Syd and Duncan were alone in the garage. He flipped through sheets of lyrics and music even though he had a perfect familiarity with the band's material. Syd spent a minute or so trying to nail a G, C, D, G progression, yet always failing. Duncan hid his dismay, cringing only slightly.

"I'm pretty horrible," Syd sighed. "Sorry. Just thought I should throw that out there."

Yeah, thanks for the news flash, thought Duncan.

"You're fine, Syd," he said, looking up from his papers. "Don't sweat it."

"I am beyond help. You make my parts easier, and I make them suckier."

You really are criminally bad.

"You won't get any better thinking like that, Syd."

"I know. But I can't *stop* thinking like that. Which is why I'm pretty sure I can't get better." She sighed again. "You know, I'm actually reasonably confident in all other areas of my life. But this one—the one that I really care about—well . . ."

Jessie and Stew returned, each with a handful of cheese-flavored chips.

"Thought you were in fit-into-the-dress mode, beauty queen," said Duncan, grinning at Jessie.

"Screw that," she said. "I love cheese." She sat back down at her drums. Stew jammed his chip pile into his mouth and chewed noisily.

"Okay," said Duncan. "So as I was saying before Jess's bladder interrupted us, we're struggling with the bridge on—"

There was a knock at the side door of the garage.

Duncan looked at the door, puzzled.

Another knock. "Who the—?"

The door creaked open. Carly stepped through lugging a large plastic bag.

"Hi, Dunky!" she said.

"Oh, hey!" he yelped. "You finally came to watch us! Awesome! This is too great. We're so stoked about the rally, right, guys?" The band said nothing. "Put your stuff down anywhere—we'll play something for you." He grinned, then looked at the band. Jess and Stew kept chewing. Syd bent the Twins cap low over her eyes.

"Okay," said Duncan. "Let's let's try 'Rat Maze Funk' on my count. One, two—"

"Actually, Duncan, I can't stay," said Carly.

Syd exhaled loudly.

"I'm so swamped with all this pre-rally stuff," continued Carly. "So much to plan. It's mere days away!" She clapped silently. "I've gotta reconfirm with the Fox crew, then I'm giving an interview to the *Elm Forest Leader*." She shook her head. "I seriously can't believe I'm giving an interview. Wow." She dropped the bag. "Anyway, I just wanted to drop off costumes."

This drew a blank stare from Duncan, and three horrified looks from the rest of the Tarts.

"Costumes?" asked Duncan.

Carly rustled in the bag for a few seconds, then held up a rat mask, a fuzzy suit, and an outlandishly long white tail.

"Hee!" she squealed. "Now just tell me that's not the cutest!"

"Dude," said Jessie. "I liked the conquistador outfit a little bet—"

"Are we supposed to *play* in those?" asked Duncan, cutting her off. "Because, I mean, that's no easy trick. A five-foot-long tail is not really something most musicians have to deal with." He thought of just how dreadful Syd's playing was when she went without a mask. He couldn't imagine what impaired vision might do.

"Dunky, we're so happy to have your band at the rally," Carly said. "And we'd really be superthrilled if you guys could wear the rat suits. Please? A lot of our members are wearing them. To show solidarity."

"This band doesn't do gimmicks," declared Stew flatly. He folded his arms.

Carly flashed an exaggerated frown, then looked toward Duncan. "Pleeeease?" she asked.

The band stared at him. Carly pouted.

"I . . . we . . . it's just . . ." Duncan looked at his feet. "Stew's

right, we are not a band that has traditionally engaged in gim-
mickry, really, and, um . . ."

More pouting from Carly.

This is not what the group reunited for, Duncan thought.
Our first public appearance cannot involve masks with long
whiskers. But I can't start saying no to Carly, either. Not
with things progressing at the present rate. *A great night*, he
thought, almost mouthing the words.

"*I'll* wear the suit, Carly," he said. "I can promise you
that."

"Actually," she said, still pouting, "I didn't bring a full
suit for you, Dunky. Just a tail and a mask. The suit is kind of
tricky to get in and out of. I was hoping you'd just wear a robe
or something."

He looked at her, confused again. "Sorry, I'm not really
following."

"She's saying she wants you *nekked*, Dunky!" said Jessie,
snorting.

"Well, I was sort of hoping that you would streak with us."
She smiled, then emoted. "For the past couple weeks, you have
been *the* key member of TARTS, Duncan. Nobody's done as
much for us. Not Marissa, not me . . . no one. And volunteer-
ing to perform at the rally? Well, that's over the top. You're
the best. It occurred to me that at the end of the day, all the
attention is going to go to the streakers." Carly walked toward
Duncan and grabbed his hand. "If anyone has earned the right
to streak, it's you," she said.

Jessie snickered. Duncan was struck by a kind of aphasia. His mouth moved, but no sounds emerged.

"I thought you were committed, Duncan," said Carly. "Totally committed."

More soundless mouthing. Carly stared.

Finally, this: "I love the mice. But, I mean . . . getting arrested? That's no small thing. We might miss homecoming, Carly. Because we're in jail. We'll have jailhouse homecoming. I hadn't really pla—"

"*Homecoming?*" said Carly. "Duncan, we're trying to save little lives. Remember?"

An awkward silence followed.

Then Syd and Jessie began making mouse noises.

"So, um . . . what time is this rally, anyway?" Stew blurted.

"Yeah," said Jessie. "What time? Because I'm *definitely* going to homecoming. With a boy—a big one. And I've got this sweet bubble-skirt dress that might get all wrinkly if I wear it underneath a rat suit." She paused, then added a sarcastic, "*Dunky.*"

Syd snorted.

Carly pouted.

"Noon," said Carly. "The rally's at noon." She looked into Duncan's eyes. "Are you with us or not? If you're not, I'd like to know. Maybe I misjudged you. I thought you cared enough to really take risks."

Oh, you just have *noooo* idea, he thought.

"I do. I care. I'm full of caring. And risk-taking."

"So you'll do it?"

What if it's cold? he thought. Like, really cold. It's October. I'll be naked in the cold. And what happens in cold weather? Contraction. Not exactly the most flattering weather conditions in which to be outdoors and nak—

"Well?" said Carly. "Will you?" More pouting.

"Yeah," he finally said. "Sure."

Carly smiled and brushed his cheek. "You're a good person, Duncan Boone. It's the right thing to do."

Naked with a rat tail is the *right* thing to do? he thought. Hmm. Well I ain't doin' it for the rats, I'll tell you tha—

Carly leaned close and kissed him on the lips.

Not a long kiss, not a tongue kiss. But still, a lip-to-lip kiss. Duncan nearly toppled over. Jess, Stew, and Syd nearly did, too.

"'Bye, Dunky," said Carly.

The instant she left, Stew clapped Duncan on the back.

"Mostly I'm impressed by you," he said. "But the part that isn't impressed is pretty grossed out. I've already seen all of you I care to see."

"What the hell did I just agree to?"

"Gettin' naked," said Stew. "I thought that was pretty clear."

Duncan held up one of the rat tails. "You think I can use this to cover myself?"

"Dude," said Jessie, "if a five-foot-long plush tail *won't* cover you, then there's really nothing to be ashamed of, is there?"

21

Not long after the visit from Carly, Syd and Jessie left practice. Just as well, thought Duncan. The smooch—quick though it was—had caused him to completely lose focus. What did the kiss even mean? Were he and Carly an item? Certainly not in any official way. There were no public displays of affection between them. There were no dates, no phone calls, and only the one brief IM exchange. It was an odd kiss. No outflow of emotion. Almost clinical. But still, it was more action than he'd expected.

Duncan sat at his kitchen table, trying to study yet unable to concentrate.

Oh my God, she expects me to get *naked*, he occasionally thought.

Then, Oh my God, *she's* going to get naked.

Duncan's mom entered the kitchen and began to empty the dishwasher. They'd spoken only briefly (and tersely) to each other since Freddie's suspension.

"What are you working on, honey?"

"My application to transfer to another school. In Guam. On a mountain. Protected by cannibals."

She smiled. "I'll just follow you wherever you go," she said.

"Like that's news to me."

"You know I had to do *something* about Freddie, right, Duncan?"

He sat silently. She opened a cabinet and began to put away drinking glasses.

"Teachers were coming to me," she said. "Students were even coming to me. There was sincere concern for your safety."

"Freddie's not what you think he is."

"I think he's a bully."

"I know you do, Mother."

"His sister seems very nice, though."

"She's not a strong guitar player." Duncan pretended to read a textbook. "But yes, she's very nice."

After several more minutes of distracted (and sometimes faked) study, Duncan went upstairs to his room. He sat at his desk, continuing not to study. Another good time to crack open the journal, he thought. But alas, Mrs. Kindler still had it. And, by that point, anything he might've wanted to write about involved people and circumstances that couldn't be discussed with a woman who played bunco with his mom. So, instead of being productive or contemplative, Duncan stretched out on his bed and put *The Song Remains the Same* on his stereo. Just as the title track began to play, a car squealed to a stop outside his house.

Duncan turned the music down low. He then heard plod-ding footsteps outside. Then the doorbell rang. Then there were a series of loud thuds on the front door. He heard mut-tering from his parents downstairs.

Duncan went over to his bedroom window and swept back the curtain. Syd's Monte Carlo was parked outside. But Syd didn't plod or thud.

"Good evening, Mrs. Boone." Freddie's voice boomed. "Is Duncan at home?"

Oh crap, thought Duncan. Freddie's girl.

If, indeed, a girl existed who would willingly attend a social engagement with Freddie Wambaugh, Duncan hadn't yet located her. Nor had he started looking. Duncan listened at his door. He heard a very clear "not sure that's such a good idea" from his mother, followed by something inaudible—but very serious-sounding—from his dad.

Well, no way they're letting Freddie in the house, he thought. Not after getting him suspended and bad-mouthing him at every oppor—

He soon heard laughter from his parents. And then from Freddie. Duncan soundlessly eased open the door to better hear the conversation:

Freddie: ". . . and I know it was wrong. I really do."

Dad: "That's fine, Freddie. You're demonstrating a great deal of maturity."

Freddie: "Suspension was a wake-up call, sir."

Mom: "I'll take you upstairs, Frederick."

Where is this amazing gullibility when I need it? wondered Duncan. Who falls for this crap?

Duncan shut his door, turned the stereo back up just slightly, and sat down at his desk, again pretending to be scholastically engaged. He soon heard Freddie's heavy footsteps in the living room. Then on the stairs. Then in hallway. There was a knock at the door of his room.

"Yeah?" said Duncan, as though he'd heard nothing of Freddie's arrival.

The door opened. Freddie completely filled the doorway. Duncan's mom stood behind him, smiling politely.

"Greetings, dor—errr, Duncan," said Freddie.

"I'll let you kids talk," said Duncan's mom.

Freddie stepped forward and pulled the door shut. "Evenin', dweeb."

"Look, Freddie, don't pummel me. Not now, when no one's looking. And definitely not with my parents in the house—that's basically insane. And criminal. I know I haven't firmed up a homecoming date for you yet, but it's not like I—"

"Enough of your dipwaddery," said Freddie, waving his hands in clear frustration. "It's like you and I, we're never on the same conversational wavelength. It's funny, because we work pretty well together when I kick your ass." Freddie threw himself down on Duncan's bed. The springs scrinched loudly under Freddie's weight. "Anyway, dork, I came over to discuss my sister."

"Syd?" said Duncan. "Well, the band's back together so,

technically, I *am* fulfilling my part of the deal here, Freddie. And the deal didn't call for me to make her a *good* guitar player. Which would take, like, a genie in a lamp at this point. The deal was—"

"Shut *up*, crapnozzle," said Freddie. "Seriously. You sit; I talk. Can we do that?"

Duncan nodded.

"Okay. Well, here's the deal. Sydney's mixed up with a dude."

"What du—?"

"You sit; I talk," said an agitated Freddie. "We just agreed to this. Like, seconds ago. I am not a patient individual."

"Right," said Duncan. "I'll just, um . . . listen. For a while."

"Thank you. So she's mixed up with a dude, I can tell. Definitely a dude problem." Freddie fidgeted, running his massive hands through his hair. "She comes home today— from practicing with you guys—and I'm like, 'Hey, Syd, how's it going?' Now this sort of casual question would normally get me, like, a ten-minute response and multiple anecdotes. But today? Nothing. She walks right past me—*crying*, I'm pretty sure, which is not like her. And she runs to her room, slams the door, cranks up some crazy freak punk music, and refuses to talk."

Duncan raised his hand.

Hesitantly, Freddie said, "Yes?"

"What'd she listen to? I mean, 'crazy freak punk' is a very broad category."

Freddie stared angrily.

"Just curious," said Duncan.

"I don't know," Freddie said in a measured tone. "May I continue?"

"Um, sure."

"So then Jess comes over, and she's all 'I gotta see Syd! I gotta see Syd! Where is she!' Jess normally likes to chat, too. But not today. So I'm like, 'She won't come out of her room.' Jess runs past me, practically beats down Syd's door, and goes inside. That was, like, hours ago. They're still in there, as far as I know." Freddie shook his head. "I'm gonna friggin' kill him."

Duncan raised his hand again.

Freddie motioned for him to speak.

"Who are you killing? I didn't get that part."

"The *dude*. Who else do I kill? I only kill dudes. And, I mean, I don't really *kill* them. But I do break 'em."

"There was no dude in that story, Freddie."

What the hell did we say to her? Duncan asked himself. Did we insult her playing? Oh, man. Poor Syd. She's slow death on "Louie, Louie" and she's no asset to the band, but wow. What the hell did we say?

"Of *course* there's a dude. The dude is implied. You don't see that? Look, I know my sister. She's not the type to go cry in her room unless a dude is involved. And even then . . . well, he'd have to be a total fartcloud. Syd's a tough girl. The only time she's acted this way before was in seventh grade. The guy was Albert Bavasi. Had to straighten him out with the Freddie Special: a series of face-flushes in the restroom and a taping to a flagpole." Freddie chuckled. "I can still see a wet-faced Albert struggling. Good times." He smiled for a moment. "I got suspended because of Albert, too—which was *awesome*—and from then on, no dudes bothered Sydney. Ever. Now that we're at a new school, maybe I need to introduce the Special to the community. So the question is, who's the new dude? And the follow-up question is, where do I find him?"

"Dunno, man."

Duncan watched Freddie for several seconds. The angry thug made thinking faces, as if the act of searching for an answer might've hurt a little. Duncan was certain that Syd just felt crushed by her epic guitar struggles. The band itself depressed her. "The one thing that I really care about," she'd said.

"So you're no help here to me at all?" Freddie said. "You offer no insight?"

"Really, Freddie, I don't know. I think the whole band is pretty wiped out over this gig. Everyone's stressed—that's probably what's got Syd in the dumps."

"Nuh-uh," Freddie said. "It's a dude. I think it's maybe that Stew dork."

"Stew?" said Duncan. "I really don't think so."

Stew Varney, heartbreaker. Hmm. Didn't fit, Duncan decided. Stew was definitely a candidate to have said something to piss Syd off. But shatter her heart? Not likely.

"I'd like you to watch him for me, dweeb, that's all I'm saying."

"You want me to watch *Stew*? He's been one of my best friends since, like, forever."

"*I'm* your new best friend, dork." Freddie stood up and jabbed Duncan's shoulder—not lightly, like a friend might slap another friend, but hard, like cop intimidating an informant.

"Don't think I've forgotten your commitment to getting me a date to homecoming either, stooge. It'd make me very sad to give you a Freddie Special—I'd do it, but I'd be sad."

"Jess is gonna help you, Freddie."

"Help me do what, give the Special? I work alone."

"No, no. Well, she might like to help you with the face-flushing, but that's not what I meant. She said she'd help you prepare for the dance."

"Teach me all her moves, you mean? Like it's *Dancing with the Stars*?" Freddie spun awkwardly, then leaped—very slightly—and thudded onto the floor, rattling everything in Duncan's room that wasn't bolted to a wall.

Duncan laughed. "If Jess Panger has moves, I don't think you want 'em. She's just gonna help spruce you up."

"*Moi?*" asked Freddie. "I'm unspruceable. I am what I am, doofnik."

Freddie lumbered out of the room and down the stairs.

"G'night, Mr. and Mrs. Boone," he said. "It was a pleasure."

Duncan listened to the Monte Carlo peel off into the October night. He wondered how on Earth—what with daily band practices, TARTS minutiae, and a landfill's worth of neglected schoolwork—he was going to be able to find Frederick Wambaugh a date. He looked down at his desk and saw a TARTS membership list poking out of a three-subject notebook.

He fished it out, then picked up his cell phone and dialed. "Hello, Marissa? Hey, Duncan here . . ."

22

Matchmaking for Freddie turned out to be one of the simpler issues facing Duncan. Without any financial inducement whatsoever, Marissa agreed to be set up with a boy described to her only as "larger than the average teenage male, but visually impressive nonetheless." She didn't even ask his name. This was probably for the best, Duncan had decided. It seemed that he had a new reserve of TARTS-related clout, and Marissa felt she couldn't refuse him. He smiled, contentedly.

"A great night," he told himself smugly.

The week of the rally was a swirl of urgent TARTS chores and band practices—hours of band practices. In fact, in the five full days between Duncan's brief lip-on-lip action with Carly and the rally—at which they were to appear together naked—he scarcely saw the girl for whom he'd gone to such ludicrous trouble. Mostly he just saw Jessie, Stew, and Syd.

And Syd, to absolutely no one's surprise, was still sucking on guitar. Moreover, she seemed unusually dour. Duncan could certainly see why her brother was concerned.

"Talk to her," he told Jessie. "She's bummin' me out."

She flicked his ear. "I am not the good-mood fairy," she said. "You're such a moron."

He was *tired* is what he was. His sleep had been disturbed all week by a mix of worry and excitement—and it was about a 70/30 mix, dominated by worry. Saturday was going to be the band's first gig ever. And, unlike most first gigs for most bands, it seemed like theirs was going to be absurdly well attended, both by the local citizenry and a few members of the media. Carly had coordinated the rally expertly. She had a kind of genius for organization. Attendees of the Elm Forest homecoming parade were going to get an earful of pro-rodent rhetoric whether they wanted it or not. They would also get an eyeful of naked high school students. The homecoming court was going to be pelted with rubber rats by protesters (Duncan's idea) while being serenaded by one of six rodent-centric songs from the Flaming Tarts. How Carly had gotten representatives from both state and city government to agree to speak at the rally was really a mystery to him, but he could vouch for her persuasiveness.

On rally morning, Duncan awoke with two things weighing heavily on him: (1) he was expected to strip naked in public on a slightly chilly day, and (2) his band's rhythm guitarist had zero rhythm and a functionally useless guitar. To address the first concern, he would wear boxers under the robe and rat tail.

A simple enough solution. If Carly questioned his commitment again, at least he'd be *mostly* naked. He could claim to have been afraid of peeking out of the robe prematurely during his performance, thus ruining the surprise of the mass streak. And, hell, if Carly really gave him flak, he could always jettison the boxers when he was safely offstage.

The second problem—Syd's sucking—really had no obvious solution.

The rally was to begin at noon. Duncan had his gear packed and loaded in the car, and his rat tail on at 7 a.m. He had already finished breakfast by the time his mother came downstairs.

"Morning, Dunk," she said.

"Hey, Mom."

"Are you so excited for the rally today?" She dropped two bread slices in the toaster.

"I guess."

"You *guess*? You were up awfully early for someone who's not sure he's excited."

"Well, if you knew I was excited, why ask? I'm a teenage male. You pretty much know I'm only going to say 'Fine' or 'I dunno' or 'I guess' when you ask me something."

"Why is that?"

"I dunno."

"Don't be a wiseacre."

"Fine."

"Duncan, will you please stop this?"

"I guess."

She stared at him with mild annoyance. Then she smiled. "Well, your father and I are excited for your show today. We can't wait."

"You *what*?!" he snapped. "Oh, you can wait. You can wait until I'm rockin' the United Center on the band's tenth North American tour in support of our fifth platinum album. You are definitely not seeing me today. Or any other day anytime soon. You aren't allowed."

"Duncan Boone," she said didactically. "I am watching your show today whether it's allowed or not. This is not negotiable. I am your mother. They pried you from my body with metal tools. I can do whatever I want to you."

"Gross, Mom."

"Your father and sister are coming, too."

The toast popped. Duncan stomped off to the garage. He stood alone, psyching himself. He put some Dinosaur Jr on the garage's grime-covered CD player. He bobbed his head, closed his eyes, and visualized an idealized rally scene: pogoing suburbanites at the edge of the stage, random acts of hedonism, excited fans—whipped into madness by the Flaming Tarts' cosmic awesomeness—flinging clumps of the Watts Park grass into the air. And, of course, the sound of Duncan's voice and his elliptical guitar wizardry. He shut off the CD player, grabbed his guitar, and bent a series of notes, the opening riff of what was supposed to be the rally's first song, "Fat Rat Trap." Duncan barked out the first verse:

Oh, I got eyes just for you
One of them's black and the other one's blue
The right one's a lie but the left one's true
And I'm in a rat in a trap and the glue is you . . .

He spun, jamming in a theatrical yet economical way, until he fell totally at ease with his mastery of the Tarts' set. He was ready. First gig, first audience. The band was ready. Except, well . . . Syd. What to do? He still couldn't say.

Duncan drove to Watts Park with the gear. It was the sort of crystalline autumn day that all virtuous rallies deserve. Cloudless sky, brilliant sun, leaves whipped into small circles, air stirred by sharp breezes. Dogs chased rubber toys and toddlers toddled. Adults chatted with one another and caffeinated themselves. Duncan lugged band equipment.

"Damn," said Jessie, ambling up behind him. "This tail keeps creeping up my butt. Is this a problem you're having?"

"No, I'm, um . . . my tail and my butt are in balance. Thanks for asking."

After unloading their gear and arranging it on a stage that had been assembled overnight, Duncan and Jessie stood together near the soldier statue, in their matching masks and tails, and watched the crowd gather.

And gather.

And gather.

"Dude, there's a lotta people here," she said at eleven forty-five.

"You ain't kiddin'."

Hundreds of people milled about on the grass. Some had brought blankets, others protest signs. The news van with its telescoping satellite transmitter was parked along the edge of the park.

"You scared?" asked Jessie.

"Hell no."

And he meant it. He felt as if a dream had drawn very close. A band, an audience, a girl. Carly was flitting about, checking on a thousand things at once, her plush tail whipping behind her. *A great night.* This delicious phrase made Duncan whole.

Politicians with plastic faces shook hands and bared their giant teeth. A tall girl in a rat mask approached.

"Hey, Duncan," said Marissa, lifting the mask.

"Oh, hey."

"When do I meet this boy?"

"*This* is who you set him up with?" said Jessie derisively, eyeing Marissa. "He's too much man for her."

"Back off, sister," said Marissa.

Jessie took a step toward her, but Duncan thrust an arm between them, pointing to the front row of the crowd.

"There he is," said Duncan. "Go introduce yourself."

Freddie turned out to be quite visually impressive—and in a good way. He had a crisp, wrinkleless shirt over stylish, unstained, well-cut jeans. His hair was groomed, but not *too* groomed. He was far less slobbish than usual.

"Hmm," said Marissa. "Not so bad." She waved, then

furrowed her brow. "Hey, isn't that the dude who beats you up? Or is that his better-looking brother?"

"No, that's the guy," said Duncan. "It's kind of an involved story. I don't really have time to hit all the details for you now. Just go say hi. He won't bite."

Marissa placed the mask back over her face and walked slowly toward Freddie.

"At least I don't think he'd bite . . . a girl. He'd definitely bite a dude."

Jessie grinned, still looking at Freddie.

"Are you responsible for Freddie's transformation?" asked Duncan.

"Partly, yes," said Jess. "He looks quite nice, don't you think?"

"Hmm," he said, not quite admitting anything.

Duncan's eyes swept over the crowd, picking out the faces he knew: Sloth was standing near Freddie, and already in his homecoming attire; Duncan's parents were there with Talia—and, to Duncan's horror, with Emily; several teachers were there, including Dr. Wiggins, the TARTS adviser, and Mrs. Kindler; wannabe rapper Kurt Himes was there. . . .

And he was wearing a tail and mask.

And he was talking to Carly—not just talking politely, but close-talking. Almost intimately.

Duncan grabbed Jess's head, twisting it away from Marissa and Freddie. "Look at *that*," he insisted, pointing at Kurt and Carly.

"Dude," said Jessie. "That's so weird. The rat tail isn't riding up either of their butts, eith—"

"No!" he said. "Just look at them. They're, like, cozy."

And then it happened: Carly quick-kissed Kurt, just the way she'd smooched Duncan in his garage. On the lips. Not with any flicker of lust, exactly. But it was still something.

That's *my* kiss! he thought.

"Whoa," said Jessie.

Duncan's heart plummeted, like in a Tower of Terror sort of way. The breath left his chest, and beads of cold perspiration formed on his forehead.

"Whoa is right," he said.

23

Duncan's head was abuzz. As Carly strode away, he saw the same wide-eyed, jittery look on Kurt's face that he'd had a week prior. Duncan took off to intercept Carly, who seemed to be on her way to corral a small gaggle of politicians.

"Carly!" he called. She faced him, smiled, and then kept walking. "Hey, Dunky!"

"What's . . . um, up? What's up with . . . um . . . well, I see Kurt Himes is here."

"Oh, yeah. Isn't it exciting! He's performing! He's so talented. Have you heard his mix tapes? So talented."

"He wha—? His wha—?"

"Gotta run, Duncan. Busy, busy. Wish I could chat!" Her eyes darted away. "Oh, Senator Feltes . . ."

Duncan stood on the grass, suddenly despondent, perplexed, and empty. Stew and Syd walked up behind him.

"Ready to rock?" asked Stew. "I am *stoked*."

"Um . . . ," said Duncan, looking up. "Yeah. Sure. Stoked. Ditto. Me, too."

Syd was quiet, he noticed. Probably frightened of her own craptastic musicianship. She should be. We all should be. With the rally about to begin, the full band assembled near the soldier-and-horse statue to listen to the pre-performance speakers.

"You okay?" Jess asked.

"Yeah, I'm cool . . . ," began Duncan.

"Not *you*, asszilla," Jess said. She looked at Syd. "Well?"

"I'm straight."

The local politicians were chillingly dull: ". . . the need to strike an appropriate balance between the needs of modern science and our cherished national commitment to treating every animal with blah-blah-blah-rodents-blah . . ." Duncan kept scanning the crowd. Freddie seemed to be unusually peeved, even for him. He glared at the band—and possibly directly at Duncan—while Marissa whispered God-knew-what to him. Talia, wearing the Robert Plant T-shirt that Duncan had given her at Christmas, bounced excitedly on the grass. Her friend Emily chased a squirrel with a stick—no small irony at a pro-rodent rally, Duncan noted.

All the speakers spoke; then Carly took the stage. The band hopped in place a little, nudged one another, and steeled themselves for their performance with nods of mutual encouragement. Then Carly introduced . . .

"Kurt Hiiiiiiimes! C'mon, K-Hi!"

The band stopped hopping.

"K-Hi?" Jess said. "Oh, how awful. Sounds like fruity drink. Hi-C, Sunny D, K-Hi."

Duncan watched, halfway stunned, as Kurt took the stage

with a deejay and a single backup singer. He was animated, juking, giant chain swinging around his thin neck.

"Whassup, EF Township!" he said to a silent crowd. The beat kicked in, and Kurt began to rhyme. And it wasn't . . . well, it wasn't bad.

Initially, the rally-goers seemed dazed and indifferent. Then they began to sway. And then their hands went up—tentatively at first, in small clusters. Then they went up en masse. Soon, the crowd was outright grooving. The politicians grooved. Duncan's parents kinda grooved, old-person style. Dr. Wiggins and Mrs. Kindler wobbled. Sloth seemed to shrug his shoulders in a syncopated way. Even Freddie danced a stiff dance—and he'd been giving the performer persistent gym-class beat-downs for weeks.

"So K-Hi's pretty good, huh?" said Jessie over the din of crowd noise.

Everyone nodded.

"Still a stupid name, K-Hi."

More nods.

"Think we have to follow him?" asked Stew.

"Guess we'll find out soon," said Jessie.

"Guys, we're gonna totally rock," said a not-quite-so-confident-as-he-once-was Duncan.

Himes utterly controlled the crowd during his brief set, exhorting them to move, to call out rhymes, and to generally enjoy their surroundings. He was most definitely *on*. Kurt exited the stage to frenetic cheers. Duncan closed his eyes and took in the crowd's noise, letting it filter into his pores and settle over him like ash. This is nice, he thought. But it wasn't his, not yet.

Carly bounded up onto the stage, beaming, obviously pleased with Kurt. The crowd clapped and whistled as he stepped back onto the stage briefly to acknowledge them. Carly clapped, too, still smiling that brilliant smile. In the distance, Duncan saw and heard the Elm Forest homecoming parade winding its way toward the park. A few students wandered over to the street where it would soon pass. And so, too, did a phalanx of TARTS with bags of rubber rodents.

Carly leaned into her microphone. "It's now my pleasure to introduce an *incredible* band from right here in Elm Forest. They're led by a dear friend of mine—a person whose commitment to ending the heinous practices of the rodent death lobby is as strong as my own—Duncan Boone!" A soft smattering of applause followed his name, most of it emanating from his mom and her coworkers. Emily, of course, booed. "Please," said Carly, "give a big welcome to . . . the Flaming Tarts!"

Robust applause greeted the full band.

As Duncan stepped forward, the moment seemed rife with meaning: his first footfall on an actual stage on which he would actually rock. He looped the guitar strap over his shoulder and watched his band settle in. Or rather, he watched them attempt to settle. Syd was anything but ready. She seemed about to hurl.

Laughter suddenly rose up from the crowd.

This freaked Duncan initially, until he spun around and realized that the Elm Forest homecoming court—and in particular its king, Perry Hurley—were being blitzed with rubber rodents by a group of surprisingly strong-armed female TARTS. This was the moment when Duncan was supposed to launch into the opening notes of "Fat Rat Trap," sending the crowd into what was supposed to be a frenzy.

He looked at Syd again. She was neither looking at him nor at the rubber rat assault. She seemed petrified, staring at her fingers on her guitar, head down, Twins cap askew. Duncan visually checked to make sure she'd actually plugged her guitar into . . .

In that instant, he knew just how to deal with the Syd dilemma: disconnect her.

He'd be doing Syd a favor—she was practically weeping from evident fear. After all, which would cause Syd greater embarrassment: an equipment problem (something that could befall any musician) or completely sucking onstage (something that befell only sucky musicians)? The latter, Duncan decided. So obviously, she needed to be silenced. For the good of the band, and for the betterment of Sydney Wambaugh. With most of the band and crowd distracted by the rat attack on the homecoming parade, Duncan rushed over to her amp, holding the mike in his left hand. He disconnected her guitar with a sharp tug.

And that was the precise moment when the rally turned ugly.

Something Duncan had apparently done—maybe it involved

the amp or a mike, he couldn't say—caused the sound equipment to shriek like a bazillion irritated gulls.

WEEEEEE-OHHHAAAAI-EEEEE-WAAAYYYY-EEEEEE . . .

It was a piercing sound, and it wouldn't stop. Rally-goers covered their ears. The rat-throwers hit the ground, perhaps fearing that the homecoming court had struck back at them with a devastating weapon. Jessie, Stew, and Syd swiveled around to see Duncan standing over a speaker, quite obviously flustered. Carly huddled with Kurt. No, not *Kurt!* thought Duncan, scanning the crowd in a panic. Carly was yelling something at the stage, but Duncan couldn't possibly hear over the noise he'd created. He plugged Syd's guitar back in, which did absolutely nothing to stop the shrill attack.

. . . ZEEEEEE-ZPFEEEE-WAAAYYYY-EEEEEE . . .

"What the hell are you *doing*?!" bellowed Jessie.

"I messed with Syd's guitar!" he screamed back. "I unplugged it!"

"Why?!" the band yelled in unison.

Carly had rushed to the stage and was soon in Duncan's face. "Make it stop! People are leaving!" She looked out across the crowd. "No, they're *fleeing*!"

"I don't know how!" yelled Duncan. "I'm not sure what I did!"

. . . WEEEEEZOW-WAAAYYYY-EEEEEE-RRR-WEEEEE . . .

He began pulling all sorts of cords from all sorts of devices, yet nothing quieted the shriek. Ten seconds passed. Then thirty. Then forty-five. Eventually—thankfully—someone cut the power to the stage.

. . . *ZEEEEAAAY-RRrrehp. Pop.*

The noise faded, but the band kept yelling.

"Dammit, Duncan!" yelled Jessie.

"What were you *thinking*, dude?" said Stew. "You tried to unplug Syd's guitar? Really?"

"She looked *horrified*," he yelled. "And you're the one who's been complaining about her playing! I was trying to cut her off before anything bad happened!"

"You mean like we make a horrible brain-melting noise, and everyone leaves the rally?"

They looked out at the crowd, much of which had begun to drift away. Only the familiar faces surrounded the stage.

"You tried to cut me off?!" yelled Syd.

Duncan turned to face her. "I was . . . well, you looked so . . . I just wanted help you, real—"

She leapt off the stage and stalked off. Jessie followed. Sloth trailed them both, but not before shooting Duncan a rather menacing glare.

You're supposed to be nonviolent, he thought.

"I can't believe you," said Stew. "I mean, jeez. The girl's not exactly Clapton at the Royal Albert Hall, but *damn*. You don't just cut loose a member of the band before a set." He shook his head. "You just don't do it."

Stew stepped off the stage, leaving Duncan alone in his robe and rat tail. Kurt looked up at him. So did his family, his teachers, and his bully.

Then Freddie hopped the small metal fence that separated stage from crowd. He looked mad. Duncan reflexively jumped from the stage, landing in the grass, a rolling ball of robe and tail. Carly and three of the handmaids raced past him, cursing as they went.

"How could you *do* this to me, Duncan!" snapped Carly. She raised her head and eyed the Fox crew, which had returned to their van. "Wait!" she called. The girls unfurled a giant GIVE MICE A CHANCE banner and raced off. Duncan jumped up to follow them.

He took five strides before realizing that he'd lost his robe.

Emily was cackling mightily, her tiny foot on the drawstring.

He stepped toward her slowly, naked except for his Eric Cartman boxers. "You . . . little . . . puke-licking . . ."

Freddie clapped a hand on Duncan's shoulder.

"Oh, man," Duncan said. "This day is just not going well at all."

"Sweet show," said Freddie. "Really, Duncan. That was incredible." He paused to take in the chaos that had spread across Watts Park. "Let's see. Your band hates you. My sister hates you. Hundreds of animal-testing protestors have inner ear damage because of you. And many of us will also have to go home and throw up because we've seen you half-naked."

Duncan squeezed his eyes shut, bracing himself for the thrashing that he couldn't possibly avoid.

"But that's not what I'm upset about, Duncan," said

Freddie. "What I'm upset about—or rather *who* I'm upset about—is Marissa." He paused. "I know that you hired me to be your bully, dweeb, but I thought that through all this we had developed a bond. A friendship? Hmm. It's possible. But at least a bond. And I know I'm no Prince Harry, but damn. This is what she says to me, first thing: 'I'm only doing this as a favor to Duncan.' She never took off her friggin' mask. How am I supposed to feel, Duncan?" He bowed his head. "Man, if you were someone else, I'd be halfway through the Freddie Special, dork—and I'd be enjoying myself. But you're not even worth my trouble."

"I *am* worth the trouble!" said Duncan. Then he paused. "Wait, no. Redo. Never a good idea to solve your problems with violence. But I just . . . well, don't be mad, Freddie. I screwed up. Not in a little way, but in a massive way. No, in a series of massive ways. I really need—"

"Hey, I'm not mad, Duncan." Freddie shook his head. "I'm totally disappointed." He walked away.

"Well," said Duncan's mom, handing her son his robe, "I think Frederick really showed a lot of maturity right there. My son, on the other hand—"

"Looks like a stick figure when he's naked!" snapped Emily. She cackled again.

Duncan draped the robe around his shoulders and wordlessly packed up the Flaming Tarts' abandoned gear. The crowd was now hopefully thin, the band had scattered, his friends had abandoned him. (Well, after he threw them all under the bus, metaphorically, they abandoned him.) Duncan had never felt so ill, so hollow. He stood—the sunlight across his face, the breeze catching his hair—and watched a livid Carly, not naked, walk toward the stage dragging the banner behind her like a fallen comrade. Her eyes were fixed on Duncan.

He tried to seem busy elsewhere, turning again to pack more gear. He heard Carly's sandals slap against the stage. Seconds later, he felt a surprising sting at his back.

THWAP!

Carly had whacked him with her long fuzzy rat tail. He felt sure he deserved it.

THWAP!

He raised his hands halfheartedly to not quite protect himself.

THWAP!

She used to protect me from just this sort of thing, he thought.

"How *could* you, Duncan?!" Carly breathlessly demanded.

"I . . . I still don't really know . . . hey, what's up with you and Kurt?"

THWAP!

"What?! There is nothing up with me and Kurt."

"You kissed him! I totally saw it! Like you kissed me."

"It was for *luck*, Duncan. Of which you apparently have none. And out of gratitude, kindness . . . that sort of thing."

"Oh," said Duncan, looking away. "'Cuz I thought you were, like, kind of into him now, instead of me."

THWAP!

"Instead of *you*? I thought we were friends, Duncan. I thought you cared about the things I care about!"

"I thought you cared about me," he offered sheepishly.

THWA—

Duncan managed to catch the tail before it connected again. "Okay, it's kind of hurting now."

"You're suddenly defending yourself?" Carly said.

Ouch, thought Duncan.

Carly snatched the rat tail back.

"I never actually needed defending," he said, suddenly in the confessional mood of the clinically despondent. "Just so you know, Freddie only attacked me so you'd notice me. He's actually a pretty okay guy. All my bullies, it turns out, are girls. You, Mom, the twerp who lives next door. Freddie's cool. If it makes you feel any better, he's pissed at me fo—"

THWAP!

"So I'd *notice* you?!" Carly was mortified. She let the tail dangle at her side like nunchuks. "That was all a . . . a . . . a big put-on? I was being manipulated?!"

"Well, that's a strong word for it, 'manipu—'"

THWAP! THWAP! THWAP!

From a corner of the stage, they heard cameras snapping. Photographers from both the *Owl's Nest* and the *Elm Forest Leader* were capturing the odd scene of Carly Garfield beating Duncan with a giant detached tail.

"Great stuff, guys," said one of them. "Keep it up."

Carly paid no attention to them.

THWAP!

"You know you've ruined this event, right?!" she yelled. "You know that, yes? There is no salvaging this, Duncan. The TV van is gone. The legislators are gone. The people are gone. You scared them away."

"It was a freak occurrence, Carly. I swear I dunno what the deal is with the sound equip—"

"I'm disappointed in you, Duncan Boone."

He sighed. "Yeah, that's kind of a recurring theme today."

24

Duncan sat in his dim and windowless garage on the fender of a car that hadn't budged in perhaps a year. He fumbled in his backpack for his journal, which Mrs. Kindler had returned the previous Monday. She'd made no notations. Duncan opened it to an empty page.

ENTRY #14, OCTOBER 15

So, um . . . the band had its first show today. Think I saw you there, Mrs. K. Thanks for the support. We didn't play long. The opening act was received warmly. The Flaming Tarts? Not so much.

On the cycle of good day/bad day that we've been documenting here, this can be filed under "bad." I've made an utter mess of a few things, as I'm sure you noticed. Today I seem to have lost a girl—no, *the* girl—and most of my friends. No, my *best* friends. I am not, as it turns out, attending homecoming. But I'll keep a good thought for the fightin' Owls. Hoot.

And so we beat on like boats, blah-blah-blah. Or however Fitzgerald has it.

He threw the journal down and looked up at the musty garage rafters. The band's equipment was piled in a corner. Sometimes, in bleak moments that weren't quite *that* bleak, Duncan would play something. But just then he was too disgusted with the idea of music to pick up a guitar, and too disgusted with the idea of himself to sing.

He sighed.

I shouldn't even wallow, he thought. I'm not good enough for wallowing. Wallowing is for the virtuous, the wronged, the worthy. Hmm, there might be a lyric there. . . .

The garage door creaked open.

"I'm fine, Mom," he said, not looking up. "Really. Thanks for checking again, though."

"Hey, rocker," said Jess. "Your parents said I'd find you here. A mild surprise, since I thought you liked to do most of your self-flagellation in the park."

"I'm avoiding the park for a while," Duncan said. "See if you can guess why."

Jessie giggled.

"Where's your date, Jess?"

"Sloth? He's been cool, actually. Drove me here. He's outside. But between the rally and the parade, I think he's already seen enough to reaffirm the decision to disengage from high school society."

"Did he say if he was looking for a roommate?" said Duncan. He sighed again, then sat up. "I was so close to having it all, Jess."

"Your melodrama is showing, dude. Get over it."

"But the band was right there, on the bri—"

"Oh, the band is *still* right there. No one's left the damn band." She paused. "I do think it's time for another name change, though."

Duncan smiled. "How 'bout The Three-Hundred-Decibel Atomic Shriek of Death?"

"That does fit nicely with our local reputation," she said. "And I don't suppose Carly will be hiring us anymore." Jess sat down next to Duncan atop the car. "What'd you ever really like about that chick, Duncan? Seriously, what?"

Ideally, thought Duncan, this is where I'd say how fun she was. Or how sweet she was. Or how mind-bendingly sexually compatible we were. But, let's be honest, none of these things are true. Well, the first two definitely weren't. And the third isn't likely to be determined. So . . .

"She cares deeply about . . . um, things."

Jessie laughed. "There're the rats, I guess. And don't forget the beavers."

"Mmm, yes. Can't forget those."

"I think maybe you liked an *idea* of Carly Garfield more than Carly herself. You had no commonalities, so you tried to invent some. That was pretty dumb, dude. What you need is a girl who really *gets* you. Someone fun. Someone you won't have to deceive just to sit with her at lunch." She paused. "Maybe you should look at your own lunch table, actually."

Duncan sat up.

Oh crap, he thought.

"Jess, wait. This is kind of awkward, because I know I've already screwed up this day about as thoroughly as I can, but I don't really like you like tha—"

She flicked his ear.

"Oww!"

"Jeez, you are profoundly dense," Jess said with a smirk. "Once you've kicked a man's ass the way I've kicked yours, Duncan, a line is crossed that cannot be recrossed. I don't have a crush on you." She grinned. "But I know someone who does. Or at least she did."

"At our lunch tab—?"

Sydney Wambaugh? he thought.

No.

Oh, hell no. She snorts. And she's loud. And she's a total disaster on guitar. And her brother decided I was too lame to beat up. And . . . well, she *could* name every member of the Faces. And she's fun. And she crowd-surfs. And she does dig Wolfmother. And when she wears that Soul Asylum shirt tucked in with that obnoxious AC/DC belt-buckle and the jeans with the safety pins and the . . . hmm. Sydney Wambaugh. Maybe.

He looked at Jess earnestly. "Do you think Syd can ever be a good guitar play—?"

"No, Duncan," said Jess. "No, I do not. She can be many things—almost anything, really. But guitar mastery is clearly beyond her." Jess smiled. "Can you deal with that?"

I can fix her, he thought.

"Yeah, I can deal with that." He stood up. "But what about Freddie? I promised him a girl. I've totally let him down. I don't think I'm very high on his list of acceptable suitors for his sister at the moment."

"Don't worry about Freddie," Jess said. "I have just the girl for him."

"Don't start cutting deals with Freddie, Jess. I'm warning you. It never ends. He just asks for more and mo—"

Jess shook her head. "Leave it to me," she said. She hopped off the Skylark, picked up Syd's Flying V guitar from the mound of band gear, and handed it to Duncan. "You need to go return this." Jess scampered out of the garage.

Duncan, his head gathering around this new idea of Syd, drifted inside to groom. He spent far too long deciding which band's shirt to wear (deciding on the Misfits, 'cuz the cut flattered him) and which pair of shoes to slip on (the new black/gray Adios, 'cuz Syd had sort of complimented them). Then, moving slightly quicker, he hurried to his car with the guitar in hand. It wasn't far to the Wambaugh house, and he drove with obscene haste, yet he worried that this would somehow be the final humiliation in an already profoundly humiliating day.

There was, he realized, a good chance that Syd would simply snatch the guitar from him, possibly whack him with it, and then slam the door in his face. He had at least that much coming. Or maybe Freddie would answer the door, snatch the guitar, and use it to shatter Duncan's kneecaps. That might be more in line with what he deserved. Duncan saw Syd's house well before he pulled into the driveway. It was backlit by a blinking green fast-food sign, so the place seemed to wink at him as he approached. He parked, raced across the grass to her door and then . . . froze.

Duncan stood on the front step in the dark, growing steadily more intimidated.

He didn't knock or ring the bell.

Strange, he thought. He hadn't been at all frightened onstage at Watts that afternoon, with so many people around and such disaster looming. But there, alone at Syd's, he was terrified. You've totally insulted this girl, he reminded himself. Not just *mildly* insulted her, but deeply. Directly. Abstractly. Intentionally. Accidentally. Privately. Publicly. It isn't possible to humiliate a musician at a more fundamental level. There is no *way* she's going to want to see you. No way. Just put the guitar down and leave. This isn't going to . . .

The door swung open and Syd stood in the entryway, her Twins hat pulled straight and low, the Soul Asylum shirt just like Duncan liked it.

"Well?" she said.

He said nothing for a long moment.

"Well?" she demanded.

He coughed. "Um . . . hey. Brought your guitar."

"The one you unplugged? To make sure I couldn't be heard, not even a little?"

"Yeah, that's the one."

"Thanks." She took the case in her small hand, then stared at Duncan. "Will that be all, then?"

His eyes were wide as 45s, his hands sweating, his feet tapping nervously. He had never before felt a smidge of anxiety with Syd—none. This is insane, he thought. It's just Syd, the chick who makes all those horrid sounds. Except, um . . . cuter somehow. And very close.

"I'm guessing from your total deathly silence that it is, in fact, all," she said. "So good night." She began to shut the door.

"No," he said. "No, it isn't." The door creaked back wide. He shuffled his feet. "I'm sorry," he managed. "Thoroughly sorry. I am every kind of idiot. I've had about a hundred opportunities to see how epically perfect you are, and I've blown every one. So, you know . . . um . . . well . . ."

"So?" she said, maybe with a glimmer of a half grin.

"So . . . um . . ." He shuffled a bit more. "I'm willing to offer you another guitar lesson. For free."

Syd smiled. "Wow," she said flatly. "That's great. And will you teach me how to do that thing where you shred eardrums with scary feedback? That was kinda cool."

"No," he said, laughing. "That lesson you have to pay for."

"Oh, I feel I've paid for it already," Syd said. She leaned against her guitar case in the doorway. "I never once cared about getting better on the guitar, Duncan. I just liked all the hanging out."

"Me, too," he said. "I don't care how you sound, Syd."

He inched forward with uncharacteristic stealth. Syd didn't back away. They stared at each other, and not awkwardly. He drew closer, his hands sliding down her bare arms. When they kissed, it wasn't quick and mechanical, but something deep and clumsy and exciting. Her hat fell backward to the floor; her blond hair fell across their faces.

After a minute, she broke loose. "Okay, I'm calling BS."

"On what?" asked Duncan, a bit disoriented.

"You *totally* care how I sound," she said. "It's killing you."

He smiled sheepishly. Point, Syd, he thought. You'll improve. I'll make it so. "Nuh-uh," he whispered. "I like you like you are."

More kissing. They moved slowly into the house, eventually settling with a thump on the shag-covered stairs. Minutes passed. Syd and Duncan tugged at each other lightly, purposefully, aggressively, their hands running over their faces, necks, and . . .

"Hello, dorkface!" called a way-too-familiar voice.

Duncan's head popped up. A deep, subarctic chill ran up the length of his spine. Just don't throw me again, he thought to himself. He looked at the floor, then tried to speak. "Oh . . . um . . . oh. Hey, Freddie. Um . . . hey. We were jus—"

Duncan peered upward for a moment and was struck silent by the sight of Freddie and Jessie on the living room sofa, intertwined. Like, lovingly. With arms and legs and hands wrapped around each other. They were utterly disheveled.

Jessie grinned.

"Oh . . . my . . . God," Duncan finally managed. "Is that—?"

"Yup," said Syd. "Jess came over a few hours ago. They've been at it for, um . . . a while. I thought she came over to console her brokenhearted friend—"

"—but she's not the consoling type, is she?" asked Duncan.

"Nope, not really," said Syd.

"I told you I had just the girl for him!" Jess said contentedly, snuggling with Duncan's bully.

"And where's Sloth, exactly?" asked Duncan. "If you tell me he's in another room with Stew, I'm totally gonna throw up in my mouth."

Jessie smiled. "He bailed," she said. "Right after I told him that I couldn't really make homecoming, and that I kinda/maybe had a thing for this other dude." She slugged Freddie's shoulder.

"You should've set that guy up with your friend Marissa, dweeb," said Freddie.

"Marissa is *not* my frien—"

Freddie was smooching Duncan's drummer again. They sank low into the couch.

"Oh . . . my . . . God," Duncan mouthed.

"Hey, I forgive you, buddy," called Freddie between the slobbery, squishing smooch noises. A cushion fell atop him.

Duncan looked at Syd. "Those two are kinda gross, eh?"

Syd snorted—subtly, if that's possible. Duncan kissed her again, and they fell back against the stairs. He took her fingers in his. She pulled away smiling.

"You're still thinking you can fix my guitar playing," she whispered, swatting him lightly. "I *know* it. I can see it in your scheming face."

Oh, I'll fix it, he thought. 'Cuz there's no kicking you out of the band now.

"Nope," he said. "That's definitely not what I'm thinking. Nope."

Syd sighed, then yawned.

"I'm boring you?" asked Duncan.

Syd smiled, then lowered her eyes. "No. It's just been kind of a long day."

Could still be an excellent night, he thought.